NO PLACE TO BE A COP

The place is Manhattan, in the year 1878. A million people live in her teeming streets. She's a bitch. She boasts 6000 professional criminals, 5000 whores, and only 2000 policemen and twenty-eight detectives to investigate all the crimes committed. The New York Police Department deals with them all — from street-gang vendettas to sex murders and con men. And they also run up against a new phenomenon — a secret society called the Mafia in the district known as Little Italy . . .

Books by Frederick Nolan
in the Linford Mystery Library:

THE OSHAWA PROJECT

FREDERICK NOLAN

NO PLACE TO BE A COP

Complete and Unabridged

LINFORD
Leicester

First publishe

First Linford Edition
published 2007

British Library CIP Data

Nolan, Frederick W., *1931 –*
   No place to be a cop.—Large print ed.—
Linford mystery library
   1. Police—New York (State)—New York—
History—19th century—Fiction 2. Detective
and mystery stories 3. Large type books
   I. Title II. Nolan, Frederick W., *1931 –*.
NYPD, no place to be a cop
   823.9'14 [F]

ISBN 978–1–84617–869–6

Published by
F. A. Thorpe (Publishing)
Anstey, Leicestershire

Set by Words & Graphics Ltd.
Anstey, Leicestershire
Printed and bound in Great Britain by
T. J. International Ltd., Padstow, Cornwall

This book is printed on acid-free paper

For Terry and Barbara

1

Lily Purcell was a hooker

Of course, decent people didn't use a coarse word like that. They called Lily's kind cyprians, or faded flowers, professional women or unfortunates, the lost sisterhood if they were feeling kindly disposed to their less fortunate fellow-females, or street-walkers if not. Once in a very, very rare while someone would actually call the spade the bloody shovel that it really was and use the word prostitute. A very, very rare while, of course.

Well, Lily was a prostitute, and she had been one for seven years, give or take the odd months. She'd started at seventeen: it was about all you could do if you were born dirt poor and untalented in this city, in this time. Get a job as a shopgirl, a seamstress, a waitress in one of the beer gardens, maybe. Or put out. At first she'd worked in a house. It was a good place, up on Forty-eighth Street and Fifth, and they'd been kind to her there, but despite the stringent precautions she'd caught a dose. And it had marked her, making the fluffy blonde hair that bit stringier, the peach-bloom of the cheeks fade to be replaced by rouge, and . . . well, it was a long, sad story and she'd moved on. Some not so fancy houses, in fact, if you want to know the truth. And then there was nothing left but Greene Street and anybody on the game would tell you that if you ever slid so far down the line that you had to work Greene Street, you might just as well put some stones in your pockets and jump off the waterfront into the North River.

So Lily had set up as an independent, her and another girl called Helen Wattis. They shared two rooms over on Bleecker and they were saving their money. The idea was to put enough down to have a place of your own. A house of assignation, as they were called. Like a boarding house, except the rooms were used all day. You could make plenty of money out of them as long as you were in with the cops, and that wasn't more than a handful of the thousands of dollars waiting there to be plucked from the pockets of fat Johns and their mistresses.

She had the location all picked out and everything. On days when there was about as much chance of finding a mark as there was of striking gold in the cellar bars, she'd stay home with Helen, the two of them curled up warm under a big fluffy blanket they kept in a cupboard, and they'd compose advertisements to go into the *Herald* or the *Sun*. 'Handsome rooms to let, with board for the lady only' was one. 'Rooms to let to quiet persons' was another.

You had to pay a sizeable rent for such a house and, of course, there were a lot of extras: linen, serving girls, chambermaids and so on, not to mention the weekly pay-off to the cop on the beat. But they already had nearly $200 saved up and that was a lot of money by any standards you cared to name.

She smiled to herself, stamping her little feet on the paving stones to get the blood moving — it was chilly for

September this year. Her 'beat' was the block on which the Grand Central Hotel stood, between Third and Bleecker on Broadway. It was not a bad one: there were plenty of gents always ready for a quick tumble staying at the hotel, and you had the crowds coming from Niblo's downtown, not to mention the Olympic Theater, and the Globe Theater a few blocks uptown. If it was also a little close to Police Headquarters at Mulberry Street, well, you couldn't have everything, could you?

So Lily patrolled her little patch on Broadway, a slight smile on her face as she looked directly at every single male who walked towards her, secure in her sense of a nice little future lying ahead of her.

In fact she had less than an hour to live.

At a little after eleven o'clock she nailed a John on the corner of West Third Street and stood talking to him for a few moments, smiling up into his good-looking face. Lily was pleased: they weren't always this nice-looking, and the

John was dressed like a toff, nice blue suit and stiff white collar, gold watch-chain by the look of it, good leather boots. They discussed prices and then walked together along West Third Street to a narrow court that cut between a couple of tenement buildings and on down towards Bleecker Street. It didn't smell anything like nice in there, but it was dark, and that was usually all they expected. Lily leaned back against the wall, straddling her legs and lifting her skirt as the tall John moved closer to her. When he touched her it felt strange, cold, with a thin edge of pain. Then she felt the tickling trickle, warm, wet, and opened her mouth to scream in terror. The man clamped a hand across her lips, bashing her head back against the brick wall behind her as his right hand brought the razor-edged weapon up in a scything, biting, killing movement that ripped the woman's body open like a flimsy envelope. Then with an almost contemptuous gesture he thrust her from him, his eyes rolling upwards momentarily. Lily was dying and she knew it and again she opened her mouth to try to scream. Her eyes bulged, her throat swelled, her lips parted. Then the man came back from where he was and neatly, lightly, effortlessly slit Lily's throat from ear to ear, skipping back to avoid the arcing spurt of blood from the severed carotid artery.

Nobody saw him. If anyone saw the huddled shape in the alley they probably figured it was some drunken whore sleeping off a bottle she'd bought in a bucket shop. So it wasn't until the early hours of the next morning that Patrolman Jim McCabe, making his rounds, happened to shine his lantern into the alley. He saw the huddled form, and then the viscous patch of blood and the buzzing flies. He pulled out his whistle and started to blow and he kept blowing until help came.

*　　*　　*

You see, she's a bitch, this city.

Everyone who lives here knows it. From Castle Garden at the southern tip of the island up to the ornate mansions of the millionaires on the Avenue; from the oyster bars and boat stores on the North River at Christopher Street across to the Charity Hospital on the East, she's a pulsing, teeming, kaleidoscopic bitch who's never the same two minutes on the run. When the Atlantic winds whistle through her soulless streets in February she's a cruel, heartless, callous slut. When the same streets sweat with humidity in the blaze of August sun she's a fat, blowsy, overblown trollop. She has all the big city ills.

Too many people. Too few houses. Too many mouths to feed, not enough money to feed them. Too many poor. Too many foreigners. Too much traffic. Too much crime. Too damned much of everything, in fact. A million people live in her streets, half of them below 14th and above City Hall. Germans, Irish, Italians, Poles, English, Russians, Chinese. Like any good whore-bitch, she takes them all on, cramming them in. There are only sixty or seventy thousand houses for all of them, if you don't count the tenement houses, and nobody ought to count them.

Nobody ought to live in them, either, but a lot of people do.

Every year the city records about fifteen thousand births, ten thousand marriages, twenty-four thousand deaths. Every year they find about two hundred 'floaters' in her rivers. Every year forty or fifty more are murdered in her streets.

Of her million inhabitants, they say six thousand are professional criminals and five thousand whores, but that's probably the only understatement anybody ever makes about her. There are more than six hundred brothels and God alone knows how many grog shops, cellar bars, bucket shops and sleazy waterfront dives.

Yes, she's a bitch, all right. Everyone who lives here knows it, but you'd never hear them admit it to a stranger, someone from out of town. To them she's the Big Apple, the centre of the world. She's big and sassy, even if they arrest over thirty thousand of her people for drunkenness every twelve months, even if there are another twenty thousand arrests for assault and battery, disorderly conduct, larceny, vagrancy or malicious mischief.

She's brassy and bold, splendid and wretched, magnificent and squalid, nine miles long and one and a half miles wide. The name of the bitch is Manhattan, in the year of our Lord, 1878.

She is no damned place to be a cop.

★　★　★

Dennis Sullivan was a cop.

His shield number was 377 and he was as hard a knock as ever sailed out of Queenstown harbour. Six feet four inches tall, he had shoulders on him that sometimes made it necessary for him to go sideways through the poky doors into the dives he checked out on his beat. He was new to the city, but he didn't show it, and if he was in awe of the toughs and street gangs on his patch he didn't show that, either.

There were plenty of hard men in New York. Plenty of toughs, rowdies, bravos who'd do pretty well anything for money except work for it. The going rate on the streets for murder was $100. Up to $25 for shooting a man in the arm, say, or the leg. For $10 you could get someone knifed. Non-fatally, of course.

The toughest of all these hard men were the street gangs. The Parlor Mob or the Gorillas, the Rhodes Gang or the Fourth Avenue Tunnel Gang, the Gophers up in Hell's Kitchen, or Paul Kelly's Five Pointers down round City Hall, Monk Eastman's boys who controlled the West Side and the Hudson Dusters who took care of everything east of Broadway. They were all well known to the police, who at best contained their worst excesses. But if Monk Eastman suddenly decided that him and his boys would challenge Paul Kelly's Five Points bravos over some juicy piece of territory, there'd be anything up to two thousand of them fighting all over the streets and wise cops stayed the hell out of the way until it was all over, because there was no way they could prevent it. The total strength of the New York police force was just over two thousand men — from the Inspector down to the lowliest patrolman.

Besides, Monk Eastman, Paul Kelly, Richard Croker — those gang leaders had a lot of pull at Tammany Hall, and the unwise cop who busted the wrong head was liable to find himself patrolling a beat somewhere in the marshes of Harlem if he was lucky, or dead in some back alley if he pushed too hard.

So, when the gang fought, the cops stayed home, coming out only to haul off the dead and wounded. Once they'd sallied out in strength to raid Monk Eastman's headquarters in Chrystie Street, carting off two wagon-loads of clubs and knives and pistols to Police Headquarters at 200 Mulberry Street. They made about as much dent on Eastman's firepower as if they'd spat at the building he used as his base. No, it was easier to recognize that Eastman's eminent domain was from 14th south to Monroe, from the Bowery to the East River. It was simpler to know that the Five Points gang owned the turf from 14th down to City Hall, from Broadway to the Bowery, and that the Hudson Dusters took care of anything west of there. Merchants, saloon-keepers, hotel-owners, grog-shop tenants, even the scum who ran the cellar bars, all tried as hard as they could to keep up on the perennially altering and peculiarly hierarchical rules of the street gangs. It was always free drinks for one of the boys, no questions asked. Unless, of course, you wanted your head busted, or worse. In which case, tell them to go to hell, and good luck to you.

Well, Dennis Sullivan was the kind who'd tell any man who crossed him to go to hell, be he Hudson Duster or mayor, Five Pointer or congressman. He was a cop, a good one in his own opinion.

He worked out of the Charles Street station house, and the other patrolmen there had begun to realize that he meant it when he said that no thieving scalawag who rolled sailors for drink money and bullied defenceless shopkeepers was ever going to give any lip to Dennis Sullivan. They shrugged, and said Sullivan was new, he'd learn — even if he got both arms broken in the process. Meantime, they tried wherever possible to be someplace else when he was on patrol. Whenever it was necessary for two cops to go out together, 'bulls in harness' as they said on the streets, the older hands did their best to pull some other duty. The sergeant, who was in charge of the duty rosters, also knew this, and sometimes took sadistic enjoyment in putting someone who was in his black books in harness with Sullivan just for the hell of it. It was one way of keeping them in line, he figured.

So here they came down the waterfront now, Patrolman Dennis Sullivan (Badge No. 377) and Patrolman Peter Phelan (Badge No. 385) together smack in the middle of the thoroughfare, making the drays and wagons and jerkies pull over to avoid them, their drivers cursing. The muddy, wheel-churned thoroughfare at the foot of Christopher Street was a hard-working, hard-drinking area where the oyster fishermen sold their wares from the back ends of boats tied stern-on against the quayside, men humping baskets of shellfish destined for the ritzier of the uptown hotels across to delivery wagons, their teams of horses tossing their heads to get at the oats in their straw feed bags.

It was noisy and smelly and dirty and crowded, people everywhere. The two cops walked slowly through it all, hands clasped behind their backs, ponderously casual, looking right and then left as they came. It was a bright enough day, a little overcast, maybe. You could see the Elysian Fields over at Hoboken if you strained hard enough. There were lots of small boats on the North Rivers. Everything smelled of fish and beer and sweat and mud. A bright enough day, indeed. Phelan said as much to Sullivan. 'Aye,' Sullivan said, nodding to one of the storekeepers who called out a good morning.

Then they heard the shot.

2

West Thirtieth Street was in Hell's Kitchen, and nobody who didn't either live there or work there or have business to do there ever went near the place, not without a damned good reason. It wasn't just that it stank, you understand. It wasn't just that the reek from the distilleries and the effluvia from the tanneries could give you a coughing fit as bad as the lung fever, and it wasn't even the stench of Abattoir Place on West 39th or its hordes of bloated bluebottles and its whey-faced, rickety-legged, starving street sparrows — as they called the children without homes who roamed its narrow alleys — that kept people out of Hell's Kitchen. Not altogether, that is. It was just that anyone who looked halfway like he had money in his pocket would attract the attention of the most dreaded of all the West Side gangs, the Gophers, the 'Goofers' as they were known locally. And if there was any way of doing it, they would separate him — or her, come to that — from that money neat as a whistle. Most people wouldn't put up a fight, so at least they'd get home in one piece. A lump on the head, maybe; a black eye even. Penniless, perhaps. But alive. Let the same misguided fellow struggle, fight back or screech for assistance and suddenly the street would empty and he would be alone with his assailant — or worse, assailants. And in very short order he would be as dead as Moses, throat neatly cut or head clumsily bashed in, it made no damned difference in the world to the Goofers.

So it was best to go into Hell's Kitchen only if you belonged there, or had business there which you could quickly do and even more quickly leave.

Like the driver of the two-horse wagon that pulled into the depot of the Hudson River Railroad on West 30th on this bright enough September day. With much cursing and spitting and sweating he unloaded from the back of the wagon an old cabin trunk, one that had obviously seen better days. A group of idlers watched him. There were always plenty of people to watch someone working. It was quite a novelty in the Kitchen. Finally the wagon driver straightened up and called one of the watching youngsters across.

'Will yez give us a hand now with this up them steps?'

The youth nodded. 'For a dime, I will.'

'A dime, is it? Ten cents, for lifting a trunk full o' clothes up half a dozen steps, is it? Leave off, then.'

'Make it a nickel,' suggested the youth.

'All right,' grunted the wagon driver. 'Get a good grip on it, now.'

They lifted the trunk and carried it up into the baggage room, depositing it on the floor, as the wagon driver gave the kid five copper pennies.

'It's damned heavy clothes some people wear,' the youth said reproachfully, skittering out and down the steps as the wagon driver raised the back of his hand threateningly. He turned and made a very rude sign with his middle finger, fleeing as the driver made a step in his direction. He'd report to the gang about the trunk.

They might want to take a look inside. The railroad yards were their stamping ground, and they made a fancy living out of what they stole from there.

The baggage master checked the trunk in on the special form he had for unaccompanied baggage.

'Where's it to go, d'ye say?' he asked again.

'Chicago, she said,' the wagon driver told him. 'By the Albany line.'

'Sure, where else could it go but by the Albany line?' muttered the baggage master as he scribbled, wetting the indelible pencil with the tip of his tongue.

'Is that it, then?' the wagon driver said.

'Aye, it is, it is,' said the baggage master, whose name was William Riley.

'Now what am I to do with the receipt?'

'The lady said she'd be callin' for it later,' was the reply.

'And her name?'

'Mrs Johnston,' the wagon driver said. 'Travellin' — '

'I know, I know,' Riley said testily. 'To Chicago via Albany.'

'I'll be away, then,' the driver said.

'Aye,' Riley said absently. He was already concentrating upon entering the trunk into his manifest for Chicago. The driver turned and went out, shooing the kids away from the horses. The woman had given him $10 to bring the trunk up here. He reckoned he might just treat himself to a couple of beers in the Tenderloin tonight.

'Giddup, then!' he shouted at the horses.

In the baggage office Riley's assistant Michael Morrisey sat on his stool, peering over the counter at the trunk.

'Jayz, but it's hot,' he said. 'I could manage a nice beer, and that's the thruth of it.'

'Oh, aye?' Riley said. 'Is Commodore Vanderbilt payin' ye so much ye can drink beer every time the thought crosses your moind?'

'No, but it's just so hot,' Morrisey complained.

'Ye can get on with your work is what ye can do,' Riley said. 'Take that thrunk out on to the platform. And when ye go

19

home tonight, be koind enough to take a bath or a wash or somethin'. Sure, you stink like wet clothes in a boiler.'

'Stink? Sure, I had a good wash only this mornin'!'

'Well have another,' growled Riley. 'For the one you had was nothin' loike enough.'

Morrisey went out of the tiny little office and Riley heard him bustling about with the trolley as he manhandled the trunk out on to the platform. He went on with his work, and about half an hour later decided to stretch his legs. Leaving Morrisey in charge he went out on to the platform, lighting a stogie with a wooden match. He wrinkled his nostrils. Begod, if Morrisey didn't stink all the way out here!

He shook his head and walked to the end of the plarform, sitting down on the baggage stacked there to await collection or shipment, only to discover that instead of abating, the smell had grown stronger, sweeter, sicklier. No Morrisey smell this, he told himself, his nostrils guiding him to the source. It was the big cabin trunk that the wagon driver had checked in earlier.

'Morrisey!' he roared.

'Yessir?'

'Get the Super! And be bloody quick about it!'

Ten minutes later the Superintendent, Riley and Morrisey had moved the trunk to a tin-roofed shed standing to one side of the tracks, used for keeping workmen's tools in. Using a steel crowbar he found standing against the wall, Riley snapped off the padlock and hasp. Breathing heavily, he raised the lid.

'Sweet Jesus in Heaven!' he said.

Crammed into the trunk was the naked body of a young woman, legs and arms doubled up, the torso humped over, swollen, bloated and giving off a now overpowering stench of decay.

'Oh, my God!' moaned Morrisey, clapping his hand to his mouth.

'Get the police!' snapped the Superintendent.

★   ★   ★

The Detective Corps of the New York City Police was composed of twenty-eight men commanded by an inspector, in this case Inspector Thomas F. Byrnes. Their headquarters in the big old building at 200 Mulberry Street was a hive of activity, day and night, for it was their responsibility to investigate every felony, assault, robbery, theft and murder committed in the island of Manhattan. Usually, therefore, none of the twenty-eight was handling less than a dozen cases at any one time, and usually, therefore, very few of them got more than perhaps six hours' sleep a night.

The city was divided for administrative purposes into two inspection districts, with thirty-two precincts in each district. If you prefer that in simpler terms, it meant that every detective was responsible on average for investigating the crimes committed in any two precincts, average population per precinct perhaps twenty thousand people.

Joseph Petrosino was a detective.

Born in Salerno, Italy, he had come to New York as a boy. His parents had a little grocery store on Hester Street, just east of the Bowery, in the area that was already being called 'Little Italy'. He lived with them above the shop. He was twenty-seven years old, short, thickset, black-haired. He was Inspector Byrnes's specialist on all crimes and problems concerning the growing influx of Italian immigrants. Very few of them could even speak American, and even fewer had any idea of their civil rights. So when a complaint came in from Little Italy, Petrosino always caught.

He didn't think himself particularly lucky to have the duty. Most of the people he had to talk to were *lenti d'intelligenza*, not very bright. He didn't have a hell of a lot of patience, if you want to know it, with the old men who brought Italy over here with them, never learned the language of their adopted land, couldn't even venture more than half a dozen blocks from their tenement homes because they could neither read the street signs nor ask directions. *Stranieri*, he thought, foreigners. Like his old man. Still full of peasant superstition, sticking to all the old rules they had learned years ago in the old country, never realizing that in America every man was equal, anyone could become anything he wanted to become. It was the land of opportunity. Of course you have to understand that Joseph Petrosino, who had already abandoned his given name of Giuseppe, was very young. Twenty-seven, remember.

There was a big crowd of people outside the shattered front of Moretti's Bakery. Two fire engines and an ambulance were blocking the whole of Mercer Street when Petrosino came round the corner. It was almost half past one in the morning, but there were enough people on the street so it looked like late afternoon, and there was plenty of noise, kids running about everywhere, the women standing together in groups gossiping in Italian, men silently watching in half dozens, their voices angry, questioning, seemingly unaware of the hour or the chill of the September night, interested only in the astonishing fact that somehow, the entire front of Enzo

Moretti's *panetteria* had been blown to smithereens.

The patrolman, a youngster Petrosino vaguely remembered having seen before, came over towards him.

'Glad to see you, Joe,' he said. 'I was beginnin' to get edgy here.'

Petrosino could see why. The kid was green, new to the area. He'd have to be around a long time before any of the people down here would confide in him. They had their own ways, and talking to the police about their problems was something they had not yet become accustomed to doing.

Petrosino nodded, taking out his detective's shield and pinning it to his coat as he pushed through the chattering throng. The firemen had already controlled the fire. He picked his way across the snaking hoses towards the blackened shop front. The bomb hadn't caused much fire, but it had made one hell of a mess of the store. The wooden shelves were charred and broken, the wall between the bakehouse and the store blown down, the roof above it sagging and shattered.

'Anyone hurt?' he asked the ambulance attendant he met coming out of the doorway.

'Nah,' the man said, hurrying back to the ambulance, his stretcher dragging behind him unfolded. Petrosino went on into the shop. It stank of gunpowder, smoke, charred wood and another more familiar smell. Toast, he thought. The fire had burned some dough kept in the back of the store.

He went up the stairs to the apartment above the store. There was another ambulance man there. He saw Petrosino's badge and stood back from the door, shrugging as Petrosino's glance asked him a question. The old couple were sitting in their kitchen staring sightlessly at each other. The man was smoking his pipe, rocking slightly in his chair.

Petrosino identified himself.

'*Lei è paesano?*' Mrs Moretti asked. '*Bene. Papa, è polizia.*'

'*Si,*' Moretti said, sullenly.

'You speak English, Mr Moretti?' Petrosino asked.

'Leetle,' Moretti replied.

'Can you tell me what happened here?'

'Nossings ahappen.'

'But the explosion — ?'

'Is haccident.'

'An accident, sir?' Petrosino looked at Mrs Moretti in astonishment. She turned her face away quickly.

'Haccident,' Moretti repeated.

'I'm sorry, Mr Moretti, I don't understand. You're saying the explosion was an accident?'

'*Si.*'

'Exactly how did it happen?'

'I not aremember.'

'Mr Moretti, I was called in here because someone told the police that shortly after one o'clock this morning — ' he looked at his watch ' — about forty minutes ago, to be precise, there was an explosion in your shop. It blew out the windows, destroyed the interior, started a fire that might very easily have wiped out the entire block — and you don't remember how it happened?'

'Is not like this,' Moretti said. 'Is haccident. One of my customer got a boy work inna building business. He left some abox here. Mebbe is got some *dinamite* in. Mebbe isa too hot inna store. I do' know whatsa happen. I do' know.'

'Can you give me the name of this man, Mr Moretti?'

'Whicha man?'

'The man who left the box. This customer you say left the box with you.'

'I'm anot know his name. Is old fellow, mebbe seventy, seventy-five. Comes in alla time.'

'But you don't know his name.'

'*È vero*, that's right.'

'All right,' Petrosino said. 'Let me get this straight. Your story is that a customer whose name you don't know has a son who works in the building trade and that this son, whose name I assume you also don't know, left a box here which may or may not have contained explosives. Your story is that if the box did contain explosive, then maybe the heat of the store set it off. Is that about right?'

'*È vero*.'

'You don't honestly expect me to believe that, do you?'

'*No importa*. Not amatter. Not amatter

28

what you believe. Is truth.'

'It won't do, Mr Moretti,' Petrosino said evenly. 'You got to do better than that.'

Moretti shrugged.

'*Senta*. Listen,' Petrosino said, thinking maybe it would help if he talked Italian. '*Siamo in America*. We're in America. You have rights. If someone has done something bad then the police will find the person who has done it and punish them if the thing was done for a bad reason. If it was just an accident, then they have nothing to fear, and neither have you. The police here do not punish innocent people. But you must tell me the truth.'

'I have tell you truth,' Moretti said, ignoring Petrosino's Italian. 'Is haccident.'

'Then tell me the name of the man who brought the box into your store. I will have to speak with him also.'

'No!' Moretti said, his eyes showing anger, life, for the first time. He slapped the linoleum-covered table with the flat of his hand. Then, 'No,' again, but not so loudly. '*No voglio*. I don't wish to.'

'It isn't a question of whether you wish it or not,' Petrosino said. 'It is a matter for the police.'

'No *polizia*,' Moretti said. 'We anot want *polizia* here. Not'ing. Is over, *finito*. I will not asay more.'

'Very well, Mr Moretti,' Petrosino said. 'You understand I'll have to talk with your neighbours, the people who own the stores on either side of yours. If they feel you have been negligent, then they may want to claim damages against you.'

What the hell else could he say? he thought. If the old man didn't mind his store being blown up there wasn't going to be a lot the police could do to make him mind.

'*Va bene*,' the old man said. 'Okay. Let athem.'

Petrosino looked at Moretti's wife. She was a thin, plain woman with her grey hair tied back from her face, shoulders stooped from the years she had spent working. There was a downward droop to her mouth that spelled defeat, as though she had been told her country had just lost a war. She raised her eyebrows, high, then let them down again. The expression was as plain as words: what can I do?

'Mrs Moretti,' Petrosino began.

'Papa says no more speak of it,' she said hastily. 'I speak no more too.' There were tears brimming in her eyes as she got up and shut the kitchen door behind Petrosino. He stood there silently for a moment, his ear pressed against the wooden panel.

'Why didn't you tell him?' she was saying, in Italian. Her low voice was tight with venom. 'Why has none of you got the courage of mice even? To sit and let them do this to you!'

'Quiet, woman!' Moretti hissed. 'Stay out of what does not concern you.'

Then Petrosino heard a spiteful rattling of crockery in the sink and in spite of himself he grinned. He could see them as clearly as if he were in the room, her with her head down over the sink, lips compressed, not saying anything and not saying it very loudly. The old man would sit there pretending not to be bothered by it but after a while he would get up and slam out of the room, maybe go down the street for a beer or a cup of coffee, talk to some of his cronies, anything to get away from the Arctic atmosphere of his own kitchen. Just like Mama and Papa, Petrosino thought, they're all alike. The spaghetti would be served late at lunchtime, with plenty of what his old man called hot tongue and cold shoulder. The silence would continue until the old man agreed to discuss it. Then there might be a truce. But not until then.

He wondered whether the Morettis would have their quarrel, and later make it up, like Mama and Papa. Somehow he doubted it. There was something deeper wrong here, something he couldn't yet put a finger on.

He gave an expressive shrug, went down the stairs and out into the street. The crowd was thinning out now, nothing much more to see, the fire engines already getting ready to go back to the firehouse, the ambulance gone. Petrosino went out through the crowd and turned right. Next door to the bakery there was a shoe-repair shop on the street level, with a barber shop in the stoop below. The window of the shoerepair shop was cracked from top to bottom. The sign in the window that read ENZO GUARDA-SOLE RIPARAZIONE SHOE REPAIR was tilted askew. There seemed to be no one nearby so he asked one of the men standing in the street a question.

'No, I ain't see him,' the man said.

'You know where he lives?'

The man shook his head.

'Any of you men know where Enzo Guardasole lives?'

There were murmurs of polite regret. Many of the men in the street would not meet his eyes. *Paesani*, thought Petrosino with a grimace. If they could avoid it, they wouldn't tell a *straniero* the time. A cop, it's even worse. Many of the people in this area knew his parents well. As a kid he had come up this street and everyone would say hello to him, shake his hand, happy to see one of their own. Yet now here was a store destroyed — by a bomb? The thought came into his head quite suddenly and he knew it had been there all the time. He'd just not wanted to think of it as a bomb, and yet there was nothing else it could be. But the only ones who'd throw bombs in this part of the world, the only ones who'd dare, were Paul Kelly's gangsters. And he knew enough about them to know it wasn't their style. He checked out the building on the other side of Moretti's Bakery. It was a small wine store, dark and locked, shutters protecting its windows. He could not see any sign of damage and there was no light showing.

Thank you very much, officer, he said to himself. Come back tomorrow and try again, won't you? He looked at his watch. 2.15 am. Just the time for a smart cop to go down into the Five Points and get his balls cut off. He sighed, and started walking south towards Canal Street.

★　★　★

The body of the woman found in the trunk at the 30th Street depot of the Hudson River Railroad was taken in a police ambulance to the morgue, where a post mortem was performed upon it by Surgeon John Gleason. He had the results waiting when Frank O'Connor got across town to see him after questioning the baggage depot staff.

The city morgue was on the street level of Bellevue, the forbidding grey charitable hospital on the East River at 26th Street. O'Connor went in through the ornately carved doorway to the morgue, thinking (not for the first time) that attaching the morgue to the hospital wasn't the best psychological assurance you could give the penniless poor who came to Bellevue for treatment.

The morgue itself was a twenty-foot-square room with a tiled floor and rough plaster walls. On entering you were confronted by a glass and iron partition, beyond which were four marble-topped tables on iron frames. On each of the tables lay a naked corpse. Above each of them water sprinklers continually sprayed cold water on the bodies to keep them as cold as possible while they lay awaiting identification by their relatives or burial in the Potter's Field. The idea of the water was to slow up the decomposing process as quickly as possible, but of course there were plenty of bodies brought in by the rivermen where it was not possible even to display them. 'Floaters' — unless identified by the Department of Missing Persons or relatives — were speedily consigned to the burial grounds.

Behind the tables, on pegs, hung the clothing that the dead had been wearing when they were brought in. The whole place had a dank, chill air, a silence broken only by the incessant trickle of the water sprays.

O'Connor went through the identification room and into the office at the back. Doc Gleason was sitting in a bentwood chair at his old mahogany desk, scribbling furiously on a blue form. He looked harassed and tired. When the detective came in he looked up, irritation showing on his face for a moment until he saw who it was. He happened to like Tom Byrnes's top man.

'Well, Frank,' he said.

'Doc. What have we got?'

'Make a guess.'

'Oh, Christ, not another one.'

'Oh, yes, laddie, another one. Cause of death, massive haemorrhage internally due to an unsuccessful attempt to procure an abortion.'

'That makes — '

'Don't remind me, don't remind me,' Gleason said irascibly. 'It's a godammed butcher's business and I don't want to keep count on it.'

'Any guesses, Doc?'

'Not my department, laddie,' Gleason grinned ferociously. 'But I'm willing to lay you nine to five it was one of those Second Avenue crotchet-hook specialists. God knows there are enough of them.'

'Amen,' O'Connor said. 'You look at her clothes?'

'Ordinary enough,' Gleason said. 'You can take them over to Headquarters with you. I've parcelled them up.'

'Any labels, name tags?'

'No such luck, laddie. Whoever took care of that little lady went to a lot of trouble. He wouldn't be such a fool as to slip on a silly thing like that.'

'No, I guess not,' O'Connor said. 'You want to let me have the details?'

'I'm just filling in the form now.'

'Well, anyway, then?'

'Oh, dammit, Frank, I don't know why you people need me to fill in a form if you're going to come over here and ask — ' He sighed, and shuffled the notes in front of him. 'Female, white, twenty-four or five, not married — at least no rings or any marks from wearing one — five feet four inches barefoot, hair brown, eyes brown, weight a hundred and ten. No body or facial scars. Good teeth, she had.'

'Hands?'

'Reasonably well kept. Not a working girl.'

'And that's it?'

'That's it. Just an average normal American girl.'

'Except for one thing.'

'What's that?'

'She's dead.'

'We don't get any other kind.'

'Any papers, identification of any kind? Handbag, maybe?'

'No, Frank. Nothing.'

'Well, thanks, anyway.'

'You're welcome.'

'Looks like we'll have to do it the hard way, as usual.'

'Do we ever do it any other way?'

3

The saloon — if you wanted to give it so elegant a name — was called Murphy's. It was a dirty riverside dive, the bar nothing much more than a beaten-up throwout from some slightly better dump with shelves behind it to hold the bottles of rot-gut that fetched a nickel a tumbler down here. The bare board floor was sprinkled with sawdust from which rose the pungent stink of spilled rot-gut and sour beer. There were benches and tables round the walls, and one or two sporting prints on the walls.

The big, one-eyed tough standing in front of the bar had a smoking pistol in his hand, and he was waving it about, the dozen or so patrons cowering away from him. There was no sign of the bartender, who was flat on his back behind the bar, groaning quietly with a bullet in his chest.

Sullivan took all this in with one glance over the bat-wing doors.

'Stay here,' he said to Phelan, who didn't mind doing what he was told at all.

Then Sullivan went through the bat-wing doors like a bull, moving surprisingly fast for so big a man, shoulders going down as he went low and hard across the dirty room, the one-eyed man wheeling to face the threat too late. Sullivan's shoulder hit the man hard at the level of his solar plexus, smashing him back against the bar, the crash of the impact solid enough to splinter the heavy timber and shake the whole building. The breath driven completely out of him, the tough slid to the floor, the pistol dropping from his hand.

'Well, if it isn't Dutchy Marsh,' Sullivan said, softly. 'Up to your old tricks again, are you, Dutchy?'

He kicked the pistol away from Marsh's reach and as he did so, Marsh lashed out with his foot at Sullivan's groin, a wicked, hooking kick that would have crippled the policeman had it landed. But it didn't land. Sullivan skipped neatly back out of range.

'Now, now, Dutchy,' he said, and even

as the words left his mouth he was reaching in the back of his belt, drawing the billy club looped there. The solid force of his entire body was behind the looping, merciless whack he delivered to the side of Dutchy's head, and it lifted the one-eyed man a couple of inches off the floor, stretching him lengthwise along the foot of the bar like a sack of wheat, a trickle of blood coming from his left ear.

'There, now,' Sullivan said. He turned round, sliding the club back into place as Phelan came in.

'Is that Dutchy Marsh?' Phelan said.

'As ever was,' Sullivan said. 'Get in here, now, will you?'

Phelan came and stood over Marsh's unmoving body as Sullivan went round the bar and knelt down by the bartender. The man was breathing harshly, shallowly. The front of his shirt and the grubby apron were drenched in blood.

Sullivan stood up.

'Any of you men see what happened here?' he said. The patrons of the dive, who had watched Sullivan's handling of the hoodlum with nothing less than awe, were quick to respond, and the policemen soon learned that Dutchy had come swaggering in, demanded a drink, then another, and then another, and when the bartender had meekly asked for some payment had roared out an oath, pulled the pistol and shot the bartender at almost point-blank range.

Phelan showed him the pistol. It was a Starr & Adams self-cocker, its barrel pitted, one of the handgrips missing, but none the less lethal for that. Anything that will put half an ounce of lead into a man's body at something like 750 feet a second is a weapon to stand well clear of when it's pointed at you. But the bartender had been given no chance to move.

'Right,' Sullivan said. 'It's an ambulance we'll be needing. And a handcart.'

'A handcart?' one of the bystanders said.

'Aye, a handcart,' Sullivan said. 'To wheel this piece of meat across to the station house.'

'But — he's one of the Dusters, isn't he?' Phelan asked.

'Aye, that he is,' Sullivan said. 'Can't

you tell by the smell of him?'

He wrinkled his nostrils in mock disgust, pulling out his notebook to take statements from the witnesses while Phelan went to get the ambulance sent down. The men in the bar answered his questions nervously as Sullivan went from one to the other of them.

'There'll be no trouble, now, will there?' one man asked.

'Why, never fret yourself,' Sullivan told him heartily, a smile on his craggy face. 'Sure, Dutchy'll be spending a few months in the Tombs if that bartender doesn't die. And if he does die, why we'll string the bugger up and be done with him.'

He turned to face the crowd of people who were gathered at the doorway, peering in to see what had happened, what was going on, who was involved, who'd been shot, were there any free drinks going.

'Get along now, all of yez,' he said loudly ' 'tis nothing' but a wharf rat that's had his head busted. Sure, if that's the quality of the hard men on this side of town, damn me if I don't ask for a transfer to the Five Points.'

He looked up as he heard the sound of the bell coming down Christopher Street, and stood up while the bartender was carried into the wagon. When the horses had clattered off he turned to Phelan.

'Well, did you find me a handcart?' he said.

'Y-yes,' Phelan said. 'Over there.'

Sullivan nodded and went back into the bar. Without apparent effort he hoisted the unconscious Marsh onto his shoulder, marched out of the place and threw the tough none too gently into the handcart. Lifting the handles, he began to trundle it up the street past the gaping spectators lining the way.

He wheeled the unconscious Dutchy Marsh all the way up to the station house at Charles Street, a growing crowd of men, women, children, dogs assembling round, behind and ahead of him. He looked neither to the right nor to the left, and if he heard the awed voices of the people who knew who Dutchy Marsh

45

was, and what this utter public humiliation of a leading Hudson Duster signified, he made no acknowledgement of it.

There wasn't one of the people who watched Sullivan wheel Marsh through the grubby streets in the handcart who'd have taken on a Duster for $1,000. Yet the big policeman had just issued an invitation to the street fighters of an area that stretched from Castle Garden to Chelsea, from the North River to Broadway, to come and get him.

So they watched Dennis Sullivan, Badge No. 377, unload Marsh and drag him unceremoniously up the station house steps, and then they went about their business shaking their heads. Either Sullivan was the toughest cop who'd ever come down the pike — or the dumbest. One way or the other, they'd find out soon enough.

★　★　★

Lily Purcell's friend Helen Wattis had been asleep only a couple of hours when she was awakened by the banging on her door. But she wasn't about to open up to anyone in the early hours of a cold September dawn.

Not in this city. She'd heard plenty of stories about girls who had, and she didn't plan to end up on one of those marble slabs in the morgue, her throat cut for the few dollars a thief might find in the shabby rooms she shared with Lily.

She made Detective Andy Nugent show her his badge, and then his identification card.

'All right,' she said. 'What do you want?'

He told her.

'Oh, no,' she whispered. 'Oh, Jesus, no.'

'Can I come in?' Nugent asked.

'Yes, yes, come in,' she said, opening the door and walking away back into the room. Nugent followed her in, his eyes going over the place quickly. It was cheaply furnished, a sort of bed-sitting room, the shabby brass bed in one corner, a table with an oil lamp, a velvet-covered sofa, a fireplace with brass candlesticks at each end, one or two photographs that looked like family groups at each side of the cheap clock in the centre. The carpet was not quite threadbare yet but thin enough so you could feel the hardness of the floor beneath it. There was a door on the right-hand side of the room which was standing half-ajar.

'What's in the other room?' Nugent said.

'Lily's,' she told him. She was sitting on the edge of her own bed, head hanging, looking at the floor, assimilating the news of her friend's death. He decided to leave his search of Lily Purcell's room for the moment and sat down on the sofa facing Helen Wattis. She was maybe twenty-seven or eight, a plain girl with brown hair and eyes, dressed in a cheap cotton nightdress, her body thin, white and bony arms folded tight across small breasts. Done up to the nines, ready for business, she might have been passable. Right now she looked about as appealing as a tin cup.

'Your name is Helen Wattis?'

'Yes,' she said quietly.

'And you lodge here — lodged here

with Lily Purcell.'

'That's right. Listen, how did she — ?'

'Very nastily,' Nugent said. 'I'll come to that in a minute. How long have you lived here?'

'Seven — no, eight months.'

Nugent heard a horse clopping by outside in the street. The city was just waking up, going about its business, heedless of the fact that the day that was dawning was dawning without Lily Purcell. A man coughed persistently in an upstairs room.

'How did you meet her?'

'We used to bump into each other. When we were out — shopping. We got talking. She was looking for somewhere to live. So was I. After we got to know each other better, we thought it might be a good idea to share a place.'

'You know anything about her background?'

'No. I think she was born here in New York.'

'How long had she been on the street?'

For the first time since he had started to talk Nugent saw the girl's head come up. There was a mixture of fear and anger in her eyes, and he held up a hand quickly.

'I'm sorry, Miss,' he said. 'She was known to the police.'

'Oh,' the girl said. 'I didn't know that.'

'You've never been arrested?'

'No.'

'Mind telling me what you do for a living, Miss Wattis?'

'Damn you,' she said.

'It's all right,' he said. 'Makes no difference to me. I just want to know the facts.'

'I'll bet you do,' she said.

'For instance,' Nugent said, unperturbed by the change in her, the rise of the venom. 'Where were you between — say — midnight and three am?'

'Do I have to answer?'

'No. But I figured you'd want to help us find whoever killed Lily.'

'You don't think I had anything to do with it, do you?'

'I don't know, Helen. Did you?'

'Damn you,' she said again. 'I did not.'

'Somebody did, Helen,' he reminded

her. 'Somebody cut Lily up. Somebody slit her throat in an alley. Now why would anyone want to do that?'

'They did that?' she said, slowly.

He nodded.

'Did she usually carry money, Helen?'

He caught a quick flash of something in her eyes, swiftly veiled, and made a note of it mentally.

'No. Well, enough to buy something to eat, a drink of coffee. But not real money.'

'Did she have any other income, any money anywhere?'

Again he saw that veiled something in the eyes.

'No. No, I don't think so. She never told me if she did.'

'Would you know any of her, ah, regulars, Helen?'

She shook her head. 'We didn't work near each other. I never — '

Quite suddenly she broke down, tears streaming from her eyes, her thin shoulders heaving. Nugent sat there watching her, feeling like a dumb ox, helpless, useless. They haven't ever come up with a way of training detectives to handle the personal grief that they often precipitate. They probably never will.

'Did she have any enemies, Helen?' Nugent asked softly. The girl sniffed, the tears abating now, her face red and blotchy. He handed her his handkerchief and she blew into it gustily, making no attempt to hand it back.

'I — I'm — oh dammit all, I'm sorry, I mean I'm sorry about this. I don't usually . . . '

'It's all right,' he said.

'You were saying?'

He repeated his question.

'No, I can't imagine it. She was sweet, really. Everyone liked her.'

'Someone didn't,' he reminded her.

'Did she write letters to anyone. Receive regular mail?'

'No. Once in a while, really nothing.'

'You think I could take a look around in her room?'

'She — I. No, I don't see why not.'

'Thanks.'

He went into the room, almost a twin of the one next door. Bed, sofa, bureau, table, lamp, fireplace. He went methodically through the drawers, setting everything on the table in neat piles. Papers, letters, a diary, he laid aside on the sofa. The girl stood hipshot against the door frame, watching him work.

'You don't miss much,' she said.

'Try not to,' he told her, lifting the edges of the worn carpet. There was nothing under it but dirt. One by one he took out the drawers in the bureau and inspected the backs and undersides of each of them. Nothing was pinned to them. He lifted the mirror off the wall. Nothing behind it. Everything that was not a fixture he lifted and then set down, having inspected its base or back. He found nothing anywhere. Then he made a list of the things on the bed. Three receipts from A. T. Stewart for clothes of one kind or another. A bill for a book called *Sexual Science* from the National Publishing Company in Philadelphia. He laid them aside and picked up the two letters. They were written on cheap blue ruled paper. The address was Baldwin City, Kansas and both were from Lily's mother. Nugent read them through. News of the family. Pa likes it out here. Awful hot all the time. Wheat crop good this year. Thank you for your gift, I'll buy Teddy some shoes next time I go to town. Write soon. Your loving Mother. It was dated February 24. The other was much the same and dated even earlier. He sighed. Someone out west was going to have to break the bad news to the family.

The diary was pure business.

There were figures in it for each day, and at the end of every two-page opening (covering a week) a total. From this a deduction marked EX. Expenses. He looked at the remaining totals, flicking through the book. $8. $17. $5.75. Lily Purcell hadn't been making a fortune and that was for sure. But she'd been staying ahead, and in her racket that was something. At a rough count, perhaps $80 or $90 over the last six or seven months.

'Did Lily have a bank account?' he said, turning quickly to face Helen Wattis. He caught the slight start of surprise.

'Uh. No, I don't — I don't know.'

'All right,' he said. 'Where is it?'

'Where is what?'

'Come on, Helen,' he said.

'Damn you,' she said.

'You're beginning to repeat yourself,' he told her.

'We were saving up. We were going to try and buy a little — a shop.'

'How much?'

'We had about two hundred dollars,' she said. 'Most of it was mine.'

'Oh, no,' Nugent said, tapping the diary. 'Didn't you know she kept it written down?'

The girl frowned. 'In her diary?'

'In her diary.'

'Oh, all right, then,' Helen Wattis said. She whirled and went across to the bureau in her room. There was a willow-pattern vase on the right-hand side. She emptied it out on the top of the bureau and turned defiantly to face him.

'There it is,' she snapped. 'Go ahead, help yourself.'

'It'll have to go to her people, Helen,' Nugent said gently. 'That's the law.'

'The law.' There was a world of irony in her voice and he knew what she was inferring. There were plenty of crooked cops, he knew. It was just annoying that she should assume he was one of them, and that he'd take the meagre savings of a murdered whore.

'I'll give you a receipt for it,' he said, keeping his temper down.

'Thanks a lot,' she said. 'I'll have it framed.'

★ ★ ★

Joseph Petrosino was getting nowhere and he didn't like it.

He'd talked to everyone who'd been anywhere near Moretti's Bakery at the time of the explosion. He'd talked to the firemen who had put out the fire, the inspector from the Metropolitan Gas Company. He'd talked to the man from gauges and taps on the ovens and pronounced categorically that whatever had caused the explosion it certainly wasn't Metroplitan Gas Company gas. He'd talked to the man from the Bureau of Public Health who'd checked the premises over, and he'd talked to the expert at Police Headquarters whose presence he had requested at the bakery the day after the explosion occurred. In fact he'd talked to everyone he could goddammedwell think of and he was no damned nearer finding out what had happened at Moretti's Bakery now than he had been forty-eight hours before, when he had started.

He said as much to his old man that night when he came home. Mama had made lasagne, and after they'd mopped up the sauce with the fresh, strong-tasting bread, finished the wine, he told the old man all about the explosion at Moretti's Bakery and the fact that although both he and the expert from Mulberry Street were convinced that it had been caused by some kind of bomb, there was no way they could either prove it or get anyone to help them to prove it.

Giuseppe Petrosino nodded wisely.

'It begins, then,' he said.

'How's that?' Petrosino asked.

'Ah,' the older man said. 'That is something that will take time to tell.'

'I got time,' Petrosino said. 'I don't go on until ten.'

'*Bene,*' his father said. 'We go in the other room.'

Petrosino raised his eyebrows. The parlour was normally used only for very special family occasions: births, marriages, christenings, deaths, the visit of relatives from the old country finding their feet in America, anniversaries. He caught the glance his mother gave to his father, but the old man simply held up a hand and raised his chin. Mama said nothing more. She didn't rattle any pans, either.

'I bring you some coffee,' she said, 'Go, go.'

They went into the parlour, stuffy with the heat of the day, and sat down in the over-stuffed armchairs, Petrosino's father carefully arranging the antimacassar behind his head.

'Mama, she likes to keep it nice in here,' he smiled, conspiratorially. He lit a cigar, taking his time over it. His son watched, deliberately not showing the surprise he truly felt. Nobody ever

58

smoked in Mama's parlour, except on the aforementioned special family occasions, when all ordinary rules were suspended. He felt about ten years old, as if the old man was going to explain carefully about the birds and the bees.

'Long ago,' Petrosino Sr began, 'in Sicily, we had lots of troubles. Religion went hand in hand with perfidy, with dishonour and with death. It was the time of the Inquisition, and it lasted until — *un momento* — *mille, qua, allora* — *secolo settecento* . . . '

'The eighteen century,' his son provided.

'*Si*. Yes, good. Until the eighteenth century. The Church ruled Sicilia with a hand of iron. Its weapon was *eresia* — '

'Heresy?'

'Heresy, yes. Someone who had reason to hate you, to want your land, to want your wife, your daughter, your goats, he could go to the Church and say, Giuseppe Petrosino has commit *eresia*. Then the Inquisitors would come to your house and arrest you. Take you away. No argument, no defence, nothing. There

59

would be a trial. Whoever wished to do so could denounce you, but you could call no witness for yourself. You could have no *avvocato.*'

'Lawyer.'

'Lawyer, because if you should seek to use the lawyer in your defence that was to oppose the Inquisition and therefore also *e* — heresy.'

'Listen, what has this — ?'

'*Un momento, piccolo momento, Giuseppe.* Bear with me a moment longer. So, the poor people in Sicily suffered, as did the rich, from the wickedness of the men of God. To whom could they turn, how avenge themselves for the rape of a loved daughter or wife, the murder of an only son, the theft of their animals, their property, their living? Only by making a means of visiting their own retribution, in due time, upon those who had done these things. They made *vendetta.*'

'Revenge?'

'Vengeance, yes. And in these burning desires for vengeance a certain kind of man emerged. Since he was a victim he could not strike back immediately at those who abused him. No, he must wait with his head downcast, accepting all insults and anguishes, delaying his own vengeance, his own revenge, until the opportunity presented itself. It might not even come in his lifetime. If it did not, then the task was passed by the senior member of the family on the female side to the oldest male in the family. It became his task to complete the *vendetta*, and if he could not, then it passed on yet again. So that it might be three or four generations later that the oldest son of a family would find himself being warned of impending death — a vine cut down, an animal maimed, perhaps. Later the head of a favourite dog left on his doorstep. And finally, if the warnings — for whatever reason they had been given — did not work, the consummation of the *vendetta* in full sunshine before the eyes of the victim's own people.'

'I still don't — '

'You are impatient, Giuseppe, while I tell you the workings of a society which has its origins in prehistory, in the mountains of Africa and the deserts of Timbuktu. I thought patience was required in your work.'

'Sorry, Papa, I won't interrupt again.'

'*Va bene.* You're a good boy, Giuseppe. I understand you don't see where all this has to do with an explosion in a baker's shop on Mercer Street. I try to show you. *Ecco!* In the *vendetta*, certain rituals became necessary, always to be observed. It was a kind of character which swore eternal vengeance, would never speak of the vendetta to any outsider. It was called *omertà*.'

'Silence?'

'Really, it means more than this. To keep silent. To remain silent. To not tell.'

'You mean like when a crook claims he won't rat on his accomplices?'

'Something like that, Giuseppe. But deeper. In the blood, sworn to by terrible oaths. To ordinary people, the men who swore these oaths became heroes. They were champions who, in spite of the oppression and terror, were worthy of respect from their fellow man. Gradually, over the years, such men found their neighbours coming to them for adjudication of problems, for advice, for assistance, for money, for the assistance of that power which the 'man of respect' had.'

'I guess anyone who could take on the Inquisition and exact his own form of revenge in those days deserved all the respect there was around,' Petrosino said. 'Hey, how about a glass of wine?'

'That would be good,' the old man said. He watched silently as his son poured from the wicker-covered flask, and accepted the proffered glass gravely.

'*Alla salute!*' he said.

'*Alla salute!*'

'That's good,' the old man said, setting the glass down beside him. 'Now the old *bugiardo*, the old liar, will continue, no?'

He leaned forward in his chair, his thin hands clasped in front of him. 'Then, the olden days were gone, the Inquisition was over. Now came the bad things. For now the men of respect used their power to oppress their own people. In Sicilia, where I was born, the secret society became all-powerful, protected by its own code of *omertà*. Now it turned brother against brother, became powerful in the places where power lies — in the offices of the law, in the Government, in the factories, in the fields. It established hierarchies of officers to enforce its rules by threats, by terror, even by murder. In all the villages and towns there was only one real law. In Corleone, where I was born, and in Piana dei Greci, in Monreale and Castellamare, Partinico and even in Palermo, their power was absolute. The mayor of your town, he was elected by their choice. If the police became too interested in how, then perhaps a policeman or even a chief of police would be found suddenly dead. No business in Sicilia could run smoothly if it did not pay its tribute, no worker keep his job without making a payment from his wage. The men of respect ruled Sicilia with a merciless hand and no doubt still do. It was for this reason that your Mama and I we moved to Salerno, and later again we came to America. Now, they seem to be here, too. *Non è possibile superare la*

Mafia.' He sighed heavily and took a sip from his wine.

'It's impossible to outrun the what?' his son said.

'The Mafia,' the old man replied. 'The Mafia.'

4

P. T. Barnum was right.

Before you ask, Phineas Taylor Barnum was a showman. He was the man who made Tom Thumb the favourite of the crowned heads of Europe, the man who called Jenny Lind, no great shakes as a singer, the 'Swedish Nightingale', brought her to America for a 'triumphant tour' and made millions of dollars. He was the man who brought the circus to Brooklyn in 1871 and called it 'The Greatest Show on Earth'. He was the original tub-thumping, brass-banding, poster-plastering, gas-filled showman. He was also the man who said, 'There's a sucker born every minute.'

Mike Bateman agreed with him.

He was a tall, distinguished-looking fellow of perhaps fifty-five, his hair fashionably long and swept in handsome grey wings behind his ears. He wore a good-looking pearl-grey suit with matching Homburg and gloves, grey buttoned spats over highly polished black shoes and carried a copy of the *Times*. He had a very well-fed and prosperous appearance and if you had wanted to count the money in his wallet you'd have found it contained around $500, which was a lot of money to be carrying at the corner of Cortlandt Street and Greenwich.

'Excuse me, sir,' he said to the man walking up Cortlandt towards him.

The man looked up. He had been frowningly intent upon his own affairs, which at this moment consisted of getting from the ferry slip to his hotel, the St Nicholas, on Broadway.

'I beg your pardon?' he said. He spoke with a very English accent.

'My name is Colonel Devereaux,' Bateman told him. 'Robert E. Lee Devereaux. I'm from Virginia.'

'Yes?' said the Englishman.

'I wonder if you'd be kind enough to do something for me?'

'Well . . . ,' the Englishman said, moving aside as if to go on. He'd been to

New York before. One had to be careful in the streets.

'You see that fellow over there?' Bateman said. He jerked his head at a tall, sun-tanned man in a pea-jacket and seaman's trousers standing watching them by a news-stand. 'You see him?'

'Yes?'

'He's offered to sell me a gold coin. Thing is, you see, I don't have my eyeglass with me. I can't read the date on it. I wonder if you could assist me?'

'Well,' the Englishman said. 'I have to — '

'It won't take but a moment,' Bateman said. 'Really. May I ask, are you English, suh?'

'Why, yes, how did you know that?'

'I make it my business to be a judge of men, suh. I can tell a true gentleman by the cut of his jib. Which was why I stopped you rather than some others who have passed this way.'

The Englishman bridled at the compliment.

'Well, then,' he said. 'What kind of coin is it?'

'Some kind of doubloon. He claims he got it in the West Indies.'

'Well, I don't know anything — '

'No, no, my dear fellow,' said Bateman, taking the Englishman's arm. 'You don't need to. That's my business. All I need you to do is read the date for me. Come, let's talk to our friend.'

They walked over to the tall man in the seaman's clothes.

'Let me take another look at that coin you showed me, my man,' Bateman said imperiously. The seaman handed over a gold piece, and Bateman passed it to the Englishman.

'Some feller traded it for a bottle o'rum down in San Juan when I was there,' the seaman said. 'He was busted for a drink, an' I was just off the boat with plenty o' ready, so I figgered what the hell.' He grinned at the Englishman, his smile open and friendly. 'My name's Dave Blundy.'

The Englishman nodded at the self-introduction and inspected the coin.

'You want the date?' he asked.

'If you please,' Bateman said. 'It should be there on the edge — can you see it?'

'Is this it?' the Englishman asked. '1767?'

'1767?' Bateman said. 'Are you positive?'

'Why, of course,' the Englishman said.

'But — ' Bateman looked as if he was going to say something else, but he stopped himself abruptly.

'Over a hunnert years old,' the seaman said proudly.

Bateman nodded, absently, as if there were something far more important on his mind. He seemed to be searching for the right words, and he licked his lips before speaking as if they had suddenly gone dry.

'Well, yes,' Bateman said. 'Of course, such coins as this are very common.'

'Hell, it's gold, ain't it?' Blundy said, truculently.

'Why, of course, my man,' Bateman said, generously. 'But not especially valuable, that's all.'

'Look, you wanna buy it or not, mister?' the seaman said.

'Well,' Bateman said.

'You can have it for what it cost me,'

Blundy said. 'I need all the cash I can get right now. I live out in Wisconsin an' I'm tryin' to raise the freight to go home, is all.'

'Five dollars,' Bateman said, as if coming to a judicious decision.

'Sold,' the seaman replied, holding out his hand.

Bateman reached into his inside pocket and pulled out his wallet, winking at the Englishman as he did so. The Englishman frowned, puzzled at this gesture of intimacy.

'Look,' Bateman said to the seaman. 'Have you got change of a ten-dollar bill?'

'I just told you I'm down on my luck, mister,' Blundy replied. 'I ain't got change of a quarter. Look, gimme the bill, an' I'll get change off of the news-stand, okay?'

'Very well.'

Bateman gave him the money and watched as the seaman walked across to the news-stand. He turned to the Englishman, rubbing his hands, glee written all over his face.

'My dear fellow,' he said. 'Have you any conception what that coin is worth?'

'Why, no, I haven't,' the Englishman replied.

'At a rough estimate, I would say perhaps two hundred and fifty dollars. During the colonial period here, Spanish doubloons like that were worth eight dollars. There was a shortage of British coinage, you see. The fact that you British wouldn't trust us with our own mint, ha-ha, led to people like my family in the South using such coins for their nest-eggs in the days before banks. And he's selling it to me for five dollars. Oh, this is luck! You have certainly brought me good fortune, my friend. Perhaps you will be kind enough to take a drink with me?'

'Well, I really ought to be — '

'No, no, stay, stay,' Bateman said expansively. He laid a detaining hand on the Englishman's shoulder as the seaman came back towards them. He handed Bateman the change, and Bateman judiciously counted out five silver dollars into the man's non-too-clean palm.

'Well, now,' beamed Bateman. 'Let me buy you that drink,' he said to the Englishman. 'And you, my good man. Let me at least buy you a small beer to consummate our transaction, what do you say?'

'Why, you're a gent an' no mistake,' said Blundy. They fell into step and walked a few yards up Greenwich Street to a saloon, where Bateman called for drinks. The seaman and the Englishman both took beer. Bateman had a glass of port.

'Can't forget the old ways, you know,' he said, smiling at his own foolish self-indulgence. 'Tell me, my man, did you pick up any — uh, other little trinkets while you were away?'

He smiled at the Englishman as much as to say, might as well see if the fool has any other treasures that you and I can profit by.

'Oh, some stuff,' the seaman said. 'You allus do.'

'I say,' the Englishman said. 'I really must be off.'

'My dear fellow, you can't go yet,' Bateman said. 'Why, I don't even know your name, and I really must buy you another drink to thank you for your help.'

He winked, out of sight of the seaman. Again the Englishman stared at him, puzzled.

'My name is Alfred Johnson,' he said. 'From London, England.'

'Good, good,' Bateman enthused. 'Bartender, another beer for my friends, if you please.'

'Sure thing, sport,' said the bartender.

'I been to London once,' Blundy said.

'Tell me what else — what other kind of stuff you, ah, picked up on your voyage, my good fellow.'

'Oh, well . . . I mean, if you really want to know about it, like?'

'Of course, of course.'

'Well, I got in a bit too deep, if you wanna know.'

'How so?' asked the Englishman, becoming interested.

'I had a bit o'dough saved, see,' Blundy told him. 'Knowin' I was to be signed off in Noo York, I figgered to get back home to Wisconsin with a nice bundle to bring to my folks.'

'And?' prompted Bateman.

'Well, I got the chance to buy some

di'monds,' Blundy said. 'An' I'm damned sorry I did now. Cost me all I had, an' now I'm down to sellin' what I can to raise the fare home. Damn things!'

'How much did they cost you?' asked Bateman politely.

'Three hundred dollars American,' Blundy replied. 'Every damn' cent I had, curse it.'

'Real diamonds?' Johnson asked.

'Sure, real di'monds,' Blundy said. 'Take a look for y'self.'

He reached into his pocket and pulled out a dirty chamois bag with a drawstring top. Bateman looked on with raised eyebrows and lifted chin as the Englishman opened the sack and poured its contents into the palm of his hand.

'There must be more than a dozen of them,' Johnson said.

'That's right,' Blundy told him. 'I bought 'em off of this old Dutchman in the Indies. Skinned me right out, the old bastard.'

'You're sure they're genuine?' Bateman asked, diffidently.

Blundy frowned. 'Whaddaya take me

for, some kind of idiot?' he growled.

'No, no, my dear fellow,' Bateman said, sincerely. 'I merely asked.' He looked at the Englishman meaningfully for a long moment, then turned to face the seaman again, face bland and empty.

'Would you, ah . . . perhaps wish to, ah, . . . sell these?'

'Well, hell, I dunno an' that's a fact,' Blundy said, looking up, a cunning look on his face. 'But you're a gent, you know they're worth plenty. Make me an offer for 'em.'

Bateman reared back a little it this evidence of cupidity and looked at the Englishman as much as to say, you see, you can't give them an inch.

'Well,' he said, pursing his lips judiciously. 'I might go as high as five hundred. If they're genuine, that is.'

'Five hundred!' sneered Blundy. 'They're worth twice that.'

'Maybe,' Johnson put in. 'If they're genuine.'

'Hell, they're real enough,' Blundy said. 'Go get a jeweller to take a look at them.'

'I think not,' said Bateman. 'I've been

caught before through my own good nature. After all, you're the one needs the money, my friend, not I.'

'Aw, c'mon, Governor,' said Blundy. 'Listen, you take 'em to any jeweller you like. I won't even come in with you. If he says they're okay, will you pay me what you said?'

Bateman pursed his lips again, as if weighing the whole matter very carefully.

'What do you say, my friend?' he asked Johnson.

'I say, really, it's nothing to do with me,' said Johnson hurriedly.

'Very well,' said Bateman, as if coming to a weighty decision. 'Let us walk over to Broadway. You were going that way in any case, were you not, Mr Johnson?'

'Why, ah, yes, that's right,' said Johnson.

'Good, fine, wonderful,' the 'Colonel' replied. 'Let us be on our way.'

They walked the two blocks across to Broadway and soon found a small jeweller's store, with a sign in the window that indicated that repairs and appraisals were carried out within.

'Here?' said Blundy.

'Here,' said Bateman. He took the offered chamois sack.

'I — ' said the Englishman.

'Oh, come on in with me,' Bateman said.

'Oh, all right,' Johnson replied. He was quite getting into the swing of it now, and it would be interesting to see if the diamonds were really genuine.

The jeweller was an old Jew, perhaps seventy, a thin old cotton coat which might have been black once and was now a strange black-green colour hanging on his narrow bony shoulders. His hair was as white as fresh snow.

'Gentlemen?' he said as he shuffled to the centre of the counter.

'I'd like to get some diamonds appraised,' Bateman said.

'Oh,' the jeweller said. 'Well. I'm not an expert, you know. I don't buy — '

'We're not selling,' Bateman said.

'May I see the stones, sir?' the old jeweller asked.

'Surely.'

Bateman extended the sack and he

watched carefully as the old jeweller unrolled a velvet cloth and poured the diamonds out on to it. The old man screwed a jeweller's magnifying glass into his eye and from the breast pocket of the greenblack coat pulled out a small pair of metal pincers that looked like eyebrow tweezers. One by one he picked up the jewels and examined them carefully through the glass, his other eye squinched tight shut to keep the glass in place. The two men remained silent as the old man completed his inspection of the diamonds. Finally, he put down the tweezers and removed his magnifying glass.

'Well,' he said.

'They're real?' Bateman asked.

'Certainly,' the old man said. 'No question of that at all.'

'How much are they worth?'

'Hard to say, my boy, hard to say,' the old man said. 'I am no diamond expert. For that you must go uptown.'

'Well, how much would you give me for them, if I was selling?'

The old man looked at Bateman with strangely innocent eyes, his whole face

79

bland, unreadable.

'Without proper examination, of course, I wouldn't make an offer. I'd have to check them for flaws. But on the face of it, they're nice stones. Good quality, no rubbish. You want I should also weigh them?'

'Not specially,' Bateman said. 'Just give me an idea of what you think they're worth.'

The old man shrugged. 'Fifteen hundred, maybe. Fifteen hundred I would pay. They might be worth more, I can't tell. But fifteen hundred I would pay.' He let the words lie for a long moment and then added, 'You want to sell them?'

'No, no,' Bateman said. 'Thanks all the same.'

'You want my advice, you'll go uptown and have a diamond merchant value them properly, my friend,' the jeweller said. 'They may be worth considerably more than fifteen hundred dollars.'

'But not less?'

'I can't see how.'

'Thank you. Thank you very much.'

'You're welcome,' the old man said.

'Come back again if you change your mind.'

The Englishman turned to go, but Bateman laid a detaining hand on his arm.

'Wait,' he said. 'What do you think?'

'I'd say you were on to a good thing, old chap,' Johnson said.

'I know it. But — '

'But what?'

'I only have a hundred dollars on me. And my cheque book, of course.'

'Go to your bank, old boy.'

'My bank isn't in New York. It's in Asheville, South Carolina.'

'Oh,' the Englishman said. 'I see.'

'You see my problem.' whispered Bateman urgently. 'I can't let that fellow out there off the hook. If he has these stones valued, he'll never sell. And by the time I can make arrangements to have the money sent here, he'll have done it for sure.'

'I suppose so,' Johnson said.

'I hate to — no, dammit, I won't, much as I like you.'

'Won't what?'

Bateman smiled. 'Why, share this windfall with you.'

'Why, Colonel,' the Englishman said. 'Would you consider it?'

'I don't see that I have much option, my dear fellow. That fellow Blundy isn't going to wait around until tomorrow or the next day, and that would be the fastest I could get a draft on my bank cashed here.'

'Well,' said Johnson. 'Suppose we go halves.'

'Halves?' Bateman said. 'Not likely. I mean, much as I like you, Johnson, I don't propose to share fifty-fifty. After all, I found the fellow.'

'I have the money on me,' Johnson said.

Bateman considered this for a moment, and then he frowned, pushing out his lips.

'I hate to say this to a gentleman like yourself, Johnson,' he said, 'but how do I know you won't just take the diamonds and then refuse to sell me my half tomorrow?'

'I'm staying at the St Nicholas,' Johnson said. 'They know me there. You

82

can ask anyone. I certainly wouldn't cheat you, Colonel.'

'The St. Nicholas, eh?' Bateman said. 'What room?'

'Three fifty-seven,' Johnson said. 'Ask at the desk. I've stayed there before.'

'Hm,' Bateman said. 'Perhaps you wouldn't mind if I asked you for the name of someone in town with whom I might check your identity?'

'Of course not,' said Johnson, slightly offended at the suggestion that he might be anything other than what he was. He gave Bateman the names of several businessmen he knew in the city. 'Talk to any of them,' he said. 'They'll vouch for me, I'm sure.'

Bateman beamed expansively.

'Well,' he said. 'My judgement rarely lets me down. I had you pegged for a gentleman the moment I saw you on the street. I'm sure you're bona fide, Johnson. Let's dispense with the references. I'll trust you.'

'Why, thank you, Colonel Devereaux,' said Johnson.

'I'll be at your hotel at — shall we say

— nine in the morning to give you my two hundred and fifty and pick up my half of the diamonds.'

'Couldn't you give me the hundred you have with you now?'

'My dear fellow, would you send me penniless into the streets of New York?'

'No, no, of course not,' Johnson protested. 'Only — '

'Don't worry, my dear chap,' Bateman said. 'After all, you'll be holding the diamonds, won't you?'

'That's true,' Johnson reflected.

'Well, then,' Bateman said. 'I consider it my extraordinary good fortune to have met up with you today, Johnson. Do you realize what we might make from this seaman fellow? If the jewels are worth only what our friend here says, we'll make two hundred per cent clear profit each. And if they're worth more . . . '

'You're right,' Johnson said.

'Let's go out and make the deal, then,' Bateman suggested.

They went outside into Broadway. There were crowds everywhere, and a streetcar went clanging by on its way uptown. Carriages were lining up outside the Astor House on the other side of Broadway.

Blundy was waiting for them, pacing up and down and smoking a foul-smelling cheroot.

'Well?' he said. 'What did he say?'

'He said they were real,' Bateman said.

'Did he say what they were worth?'

'He said they were real,' repeated Bateman deliberately. 'But not top-quality stones. Many of them were flawed, or chipped. He said they were passable.'

'Passable?' said Blundy loudly. 'You mean I've been took?'

'Now see here, my good fellow, keep your voice down,' Bateman said. 'He said they were worth about what I offered you: five hundred.'

'Five hundred!' Blundy said. He spat on the sidewalk. 'Well, I guess at that I'm ahead. If I had that Dutchman here now, damme if I — '

'Five hundred,' Bateman said. 'That's the offer.'

'I'll take it,' Blundy snapped, looking

venomously at both of them, as if it were their fault he had been swindled in the Indies.

Johnson took out his wallet. It was a crocodile leather wallet with his initials AJ embossed upon it in gold letters. It contained his passport and some other documents. He turned away slightly from both men and counted out ten fifty-dollar bills.

'Here,' he said.

'Here's your diamonds,' Blundy said, handing him the chamois sack. 'I guess I got to thank you gents. At least this way I get back to Wisconsin.'

'Have a good trip,' Bateman said.

'Sure will,' Blundy grinned. He stuffed the money into his jacket pocket and stalked off down the street. Bateman turned to the Englishman and clapped him on the shoulder.

'By George, Johnson,' he said. 'You carried that off well!'

'I did?' Johnson said. Then, 'Yes, I did, didn't I?'

'Never batted an eyelid,' Bateman said. 'Man after my own heart. By George, we'll have a dinner to remember tomorrow evening! We'll go to Delmonico's. Have you ever been there?'

'Well, no,' Johnson admitted. 'It's a bit — '

'Expensive?' laughed Bateman. 'But my dear fellow, you'll be five hundred dollars to the good tomorrow!'

'That's right,' Johnson said. He was wondering how to get away from this jovial idiot and put the diamonds into a safe place. He had, of course, absolutely no intention of sharing his fortune with Colonel Devereaux or anybody else. So he bade the distinguished-looking old man a hasty farewell, shaking his hand vigorously and once more assuring him that they would, indeed, meet and share their spoils on the morrow. Then he was off into the crowds on Broadway, scurrying up towards Broome Street and the St Nicholas Hotel.

Bateman watched him go with a slight smile touching his lips. Then he went around the corner of Vesey Street and walked across to Printing House Square. Blundy was waiting for him in a saloon on Nassau Street. He pushed the waiting port wine along the bar as he saw Bateman come in.

'Have a drink, 'Colonel',' Blundy grinned.

'My dear fellow,' Bateman said. 'How kind.'

They went across to a booth, where Blundy produced Johnson's ten fifties. It was the work of a moment to divide them. Then they raised their glasses in a silent toast to all the mugs that had been, all the mugs that were and all the mugs that were to be. Truly, there was one born every minute.

★ ★ ★

The man in the hotel room smiled.

It would soon be dark. It was good, the dark was good. There were so many good places when it was dark. He would go — he frowned. He would go — well, somewhere, anywhere. It didn't matter. They were everywhere. 'I will shew unto thee the judgement of the great whore that sitteth upon many waters,' he whispered. Filth. Whore. Bitch. There was a faint red light in the back of his mind, a slowly burning, gradually building fire. He knew how to nurse it to blinding flame. It came more often these days than before. He liked it. It made him feel warm, and strong and powerful and brave and totally, utterly indestructible. So he sat crouched on the sagging bed in the sad brown room, the flies buzzing around the remains of the meal he had eaten. Still as a sated tiger he saw, only the burning eyes staring, staring inwardly into the depths of something only he knew existed. He was quite a handsome man at first glance. Broad shoulders, firm skin, no pouching yet despite the forty-three years, hair dark and strong, dressed in a decent blue broadcloth with white shirt and good boots. His starched white collar lay on top of the bureau along with the dark-blue tie and the heavy gold watch and chain that Mama had given him the year after Papa died.

After a while he frowned.

There was something he had to do before he went out. Something he had decided earlier. It was about the woman, the scarlet bitch-whore of Babylon. No one remembered anything any more, that was the trouble. No one does what they ought to do, he thought, meaning himself. He has to do it, he thought, then. It is a mission only he can fulfil. But what was it he had to do first? Then he remembered.

There had been nothing in the papers about her, that one, the one he had done it to, the scarlet Jezebel. Nobody knew what he had done. And they must know. All of them must know. All of them must walk in terrible fear knowing that he was perhaps the next one they would meet. And do it with. It.

His hand reached out absently and toyed with the open razor on the bed. Yes, he thought. His fingers were long, strong, well-shaped. He had nice hands.

He got the paper he had bought at the shop and the cheap steel-nibbed pen. Frowning as he hunched over the paper, he started to write.

This time they will know about him, he thought. This time it will be in the papers.

The instrument of the Lord was in the land, and death would stalk the squalid streets of Sodom soon again.

His breathing came faster as he thought of it.

★ ★ ★

Salvatore Carmeli was fifty-seven years of age. He was a stooped, wiry man who had come to New York five years earlier, bringing with him the money he had received for the sale of the smallholding that had belonged to his family for all the generations anyone could remember, a little four-roomed house in Campania, about thirty-five miles from Naples. With the money he had bought the little store at 337 Mulberry Street, setting himself up in the trade he had always pursued from necessity in the old country, the repairing of shoes. His shop fittings were simple to the point of austerity: a bench, a vice, boxes for nails, sheets of leather, good sharp steel knives, hammers, a stout treadle sewing machine for stitching the soles to the uppers, and shelves on which to stack the repaired shoes until they were called for. He marked each pair on the heels with a number, and then opposite the number in the book on the bench next to his single-drawer cash box he entered the name of the owner of the shoes. He was a simple man, and it was a simple system. Like all simple systems it worked very well and Salvatore Carmeli was making a living. There was no way he was ever going to get rich, but he didn't mind that. Compared with the never-ending, grinding poverty of the dusty yellow fields of southern Italy, life on Mulberry Street was Paradise indeed. He had his friendly neighbours, enough money to take a glass of wine with his cronies, play *vocce* on Sundays after Mass, or chess in one of the cafés nearby. He had his own two rooms and kitchen above the shop, which he reached via a staircase in back. A comfortable chair, a comfortable bed, a good wife who cooked well — a man could not ask for more of life than that, could he? Well, maybe. Maybe a man could have asked for sons, perhaps he could have asked for that blessing, too. But Graziella had never borne a child. The priest in Trastemontella had told them it was the will of God. *Forse*.

Now he sat hunched over his bench, hands gnarled, stained with dye, scarred by nails and hammer and the work of five decades on the unyielding land. His cheek bulged with the small nails he used to tack down the soles and heels, making his face even more like that of a squirrel carrying nuts. He looked up as two men came into the shop. He frowned momentarily. They did not look like local people. They had on dark suits that shade too good a quality, their dark faces that fraction too well barbered. He always judged people by their shoes. You often found that a well-turned-out man who looked quite prosperous would be wearing down-at-heel shoes, or unshined, shabby, cheap, cracked shoes that betrayed his façade, told you he was putting on what the Americans called a 'front'. These men had on very fine quality leather shoes, shining dully from much polishing.

'Gentlemen?' he said, in Italian, his hammer working away bangabangabang.

'Mr Carmeli,' the taller of the two said. It wasn't a question.

'What can I do for you?' Carmeli asked. He kept on working.

'It's about your store, Mr Carmeli,' the second man said. He was thickset, his closely shaven face pockmarked as if he'd had smallpox as a child. He had thick lips that he kept running the tip of his tongue across.

'What's about the store?' He'd show them he could speak American, too.

'It doesn't look safe,' the first one said.

'Shoe repairing, that can be a dangerous business,' the second added.

'Shoe repairing? Dangerous?' Carmeli said. He was so surprised he stopped working, laying down the hammer on the bench and looking at the two men in astonishment. 'What you talk about? What you want here, anyway, eh?'

'Take it easy, Mr Carmeli,' the first man said. He held up a thin, well-manicured hand. 'We're here to help you.'

'Help me?' Carmeli said. 'How you help me?'

'We protect you against accidents,' the thickset one said. 'Against anything happening to your store. Or you.'

'Protect me?' Carmeli asked, his voice rising with anger. 'You no protect me! I protect myself. All my life I protect myself!'

'You know Moretti's Bakery, up on Mercer, Mr Carmeli?'

'Moretti, sure I know Mo — ' The meaning dawned on Carmeli and he looked at the two men for a long, long moment, their intent, the reason for their visit, all of it coming together in his mind.

'So,' he said. 'How much?'

'Not a lot, Mr Carmeli,' the thickset one said.

'We'll say twenty dollars a month,' the first added.

Twenty dollars? Twenty dollars? Carmeli was speechless with anger, and he got to his feet, his gnarled old hands clenching into fists. He was far too angry even to think of being afraid.

'Twenty dollars?' he screeched. 'Twenty dollars, no! Two dollars, no! Twenty cents, no! No money! Nothing! Get yourself out of this place pretty quick or I calla police! You hear me! Get — '

'Easy, there, Papa,' the thickset man said. With seemingly no effort he forced Carmeli back into his seated position by placing a massive paw on the older man's shoulder and pushing him down.

'You wouldn't want to do anything silly,' the thin-faced one said. 'You might end up wishing you hadn't.'

'Man like you,' the thickset one said, reflectively. 'Anything happens to his hands he can't work, he's out of business.'

He looked at the other man, who grinned. He leaned over and picked up the hammer Carmeli had been working with.

'Nice tools you got here, Carmeli,' he said. He tried the hammer out on the boot that was still fitted on to the castiron last, bangabangabang. 'Very nice.'

'Yeah,' the thickset one said. He came very fast around the counter and held Carmeli's right arm in a grip that the old

96

man had no hope of breaking, forcing the gnarled hand flat on the bench, the fingers spreading under the remorseless pressure.

'Right,' he said.

Bangabangabangabangabang went the hammer and the old man screamed as all the bones in his brittle right hand were mashed and flattened and smeared against the rough wooden worktop of his bench. He fell to the floor moaning with agony as his wife ran down the stairs, having heard his scream. By the time she got into the store both the men had completely disappeared.

5

They had a joke locally about Misery Row.

Some people, they said, their faces straight, called it the ass-hole of the world. Others, they added for the punch line, told the truth. Misery Row wasn't its real name, of course. Technically, it was the two blocks of Tenth Avenue between 17th and 19th Streets on the West Side. Geographically it was two city blocks. Visually it was a shanty slum, broken-down old tenement houses and pawnbrokers' shops, clapped-out old buildings which housed bucket shops and gin mills, barber shops and ship chandlers, card and job print shops, drug brokers, sign painters, carpenter shops, butcheries, bakeries and secondhand clothing shops. The muddy width of Tenth itself was for ever crammed with teeming, aimless people hurrying here, or there, or nowhere at all, and pushcarts lined the sidewalks. You could buy fruit or cheese or eggs or vegetables from the pushcarts or, if you were one of the nimbler street sparrows, you could live by stealing from them. That was, of course, if you weren't run down by the lumbering drays, the racketing railroad wagons, the lurching brewery carts that plied the streets and avenues from five in the morning until late at night.

Paddy the Priest's saloon was on Misery Row.

That was if you wanted to call it by so complete a misnomer. People of higher sensibilities would have called it a dive, a deadfall or a bucket shop: the kind of place that no respectable person would ever be seen in. Of course, there weren't too many of those on Tenth Avenue. Mostly they were Irish workmen, navvies, labourers, railroad yardmen, seamen, thieves and other flotsam who spent their lives working for enough money to feed their usually huge families and trying to stay alive.

Paddy had come over from Wicklow in '68, and worked hard for six years, saving every penny until he had enough to put down a month's rent on the cellar room in which he opened his bar. It was at first a dark and dank place, but the rough wooden bar he had knocked together with his own two hands when he first opened had now been replaced by a substantial mahogany affair that he had bought when they had held a fire sale on the equipment of a tonier joint over on Sixth. It had a brass rail which he kept industriously polished, and Paddy — whose real name was Patrick Aloysius Muldoon — had soon established what was for Misery Row a decent reputation for serving grog which, if it was no better than it had to be, was certainly no worse than stuff you'd pay twice the price for over in the Tenderloin. Once you got used to his penchant for quoting you homilies from the Good Book — Paddy had once been an altar boy in the Old Country and it had stuck in his mind — Paddy's was all right. Of course, you had to pick your time to drink there. For instance, between eleven and midday you made very sure that you weren't in any trouble with the

Dusters. If you were, you gave Paddy's a wide berth, for it was between those hours that you'd always find the leaders of the gang at the far end of the bar, arguing over their spoils, splitting the proceeds of whatever they'd stolen and sold, and spending it thriftlessly on the rye whisky that Paddy kept in their 'special bottle' and served to no one else. At least, that was what the Dusters thought, and Paddy wasn't about to tell them that he filled their bottle from the same barrel out of which he served any man who came in through the doors. They thought it was different; and that, surely, was enough.

'I say we kill the bugger,' 'Stumpy' Mallarkey was saying, angrily. He was a short, barrel-shaped fellow of about twenty-three, sporting the red shirt and white neckerchief which were the badge of the Dusters. He banged his fist down on the bar to emphasize his statement.

'Nah,' said Newburgh Gallagher. 'I don't fancy doin' a jig at the end of a rope down in the Tombs for that.'

'Well,' Stumpy said. 'We have to do

something and that's for sure.'

'I'm with Stumpy,' Marty Brennan said. 'We can't let the bugger walk roughshod over any man of us, or we'll be the laughin' stock everywhere.'

Marty Brennan was one of the leading members of the Hudson Dusters. Even in their ranks, his flaming rages when aroused were regarded with some awe, and his utter contempt for any kind of physical danger was held in the highest esteem by every tough from Chambers to 14th. An inspired fighter, a shameless thief and a natural leader, Marty's opinion was always sought in matters of policy concerning the Dusters. It was for this reason that he was in Paddy the Priest's saloon this morning, attending the council of war that had been convened to discuss the activities of Patrol man Dennis Sullivan, Badge No. 377, and his summary treatment of Dutchy Marsh a few days before.

'Well, then,' Stumpy said, nodding at this confirmation of his original intention. 'What about it?'

'Meself, I think it's an example we

ought to be makin' of him,' said Happy Jack Mullraney. The others turned to hear his opinion, for while Brennan's ideas were always respected on account of his deeds, Happy Jack's were even more seriously considered because he had the smattering of an education, and had the reputation of being something of an intellectual. Happy Jack had been seen reading books once or twice, which was a hell of an unusual pastime on Tenth Avenue. He was a tall, thin man, nearing thirty now, and his nickname came from the fact that one side of his face was paralysed, giving him the peculiar, constantly smiling appearance that so often misled people into thinking he was a cheerful and open-hearted soul. In fact Happy Jack was just somewhere this side of being a complete criminal psychopath, and his Duster pals knew only too well that Happy Jack would cut your throat for nothing more than making some smart-ass remark about his face.

'An example, is it?' asked Newburgh Gallagher. 'And how, might I ask?'

'Easy enough,' Mullraney said.

'Give us another round here, Paddy,' Stumpy called. Paddy came down the length of the bar and poured the drinks. The assembled Dusters fell completely silent as he did so. There was no talking in front of any outsider about Duster business, and God help anyone who seemed to be trying to eavesdrop, either. Paddy finished pouring and put the bottle down, making a noisy ritual of going back to his own end of the bar, and getting on with the intensely interesting job, apparently requiring his total concentration, of polishing the stacked glasses there.

'We'll set the bastard up,' Happy Jack said. 'And then we'll give it to him.'

'And how will we do that, Jack?' asked Brennan.

'He ain't so thick as to come down here alone,' pointed out Gallagher.

'And he's as hard as any of us,' added Mallarkey.

Happy Jack glared at him, and Mallarkey quailed.

'Is he now?' Happy Jack smiled. Nobody really thought he was actually smiling, of course. They knew him better than that.

'Savin' your mark, of course,' smirked Mallarkey, sweating.

'Aye,' Happy Jack said absently. He was in a good mood this morning, so he decided to let the slight pass as nothing more than a minor oversight on Stumpy's part. Stumpy wasn't too bright, anyway; everyone knew that.

'I'd say the man we need for this job is One-Lung Curran,' Happy Jack said.

★　★　★

Frank O'Connor was a big man, something over six feet two inches tall, with broad shoulders and the slim waist of an athlete. He was not a handsome man: in fact one or two people (who, mind you, had no reason to like him since he was putting the arm on them at the time) had made distinctly uncomplimentary remarks about his face. One of them had said it looked like a broken-in packing case. The other had compared it to seven miles of bad road.

Actually, it wasn't that bad. Beneath a widow's peak of black, tightly curling hair O'Connor's forehead was broad, his brows as heavy and black as his hair. His nose, alas, was busted every kind of which way, the result of far too fervent defence of smaller kids on the lower East Side when he was growing up. The jaw was jutting and determined, and there was no hint of fullness in his lips, yet Frank O'Connor's eyes were usually cheerful enough, bright and blue. Only when you were facing him in combat, either armed or otherwise, did you experience the chilling realization that they could narrow and become as hard and unrelenting as the shifting polar ice in some Arctic sea.

The clerk in the Grand Central Hotel thought he was rather handsome, but then he was a rather effeminate clerk, who lived alone with his mother on East 49th Street and was studying Greek history.

'No, sir,' he said, firmly. 'I'm sure I've never seen the lady.'

'She was no lady,' O'Connor said. 'She was a whore.'

The clerk flushed, and looked rapidly to the right and left to make sure no patron — and especially no female patron — of the hotel had heard the awful word.

'Sir,' he hissed, shaking an admonitory finger. '*Please!*'

'But you haven't seen her?' O'Connor persisted. 'Ever?'

'No, sir,' the clerk, whose name was Henry Mortimer, replied. 'We never let *that* sort in here.'

'How do you know?' Andy Nugent put in.

'How do I know what?'

'That they're *that* sort?'

'You can tell,' hissed the clerk, leaning forward. 'You can always tell.'

'How?' asked O'Connor. His voice was only mildly curious.

'Oh, you know,' Mortimer replied.

'No, I don't,' O'Connor said. 'Tell me.'

'Cheap,' Mortimer said. 'They're as cheap as can be. Everyone knows.'

'And you can tell, just by looking at them, that it?'

'Exactly. After all, it's my job to know.'

'Of course. And naturally, you wouldn't

let a whore come in through the door, right?'

'Absolutely.'

'Then what's that one doing over there by the cigar stand?'

'What?' gasped Mortimer. 'Where?'

'Over there by the cigar stand,' Nugent said. 'That's Katy Morris. We know her quite well. Wait, I'll go bring her over.'

'Oh, no, please — ' Mortimer said, but Nugent was gone.

He touched the young woman in the black and red dress standing by the cigar stand on the elbow and she turned, a smile forming on her face which fell apart as she saw who it was.

'Oh, Christ,' she said resignedly.

'You going to throw me in the pokey, copper?'

'Mind your manners, now, Katy,' Nugent said, 'and maybe I won't. Katy, this is Mr Mortimer. Mr Henry Mortimer.'

'I know that,' Katy said, angrily. 'What is all this?'

'You know Mr Mortimer, Katy?' asked O'Connor, amazement in his voice.

'Sure I do,' Katy said. 'All the girls know Henry. He's a little cuddly honey-bear, ain't you, Henry?'

Mortimer's face was scarlet, and he looked as if he might be praying for the ground to open up and swallow him. So far, however, New York had never had such an earthquake, and so he was out of luck. Instead he stood there, eyes bulging, mouth working, and absolutely no place to go.

'Tut, tut,' O'Connor said. 'Henry, have you been lying to us?'

Henry gulped. 'I never saw her before — '

'Whaaaaat?' Katy shrilled. Several people in the busy lobby turned at the sound, gentlemen with curling side-whiskers shaking their heads at the way standards were going down in the better hotels these days. 'Never seen me, you little pip-squeak? Why you takes two dollars a week off me so I can come in here when I wants!'

'The woman is lying,' Henry said, rearing back and standing on what tatters were left of his dignity. 'You can't take the

109

word of a — a — '

'A what?'

'A woman like that,' Mortimer finished. 'She's obviously — '

'Not the sort you allow in here,' Nugent said. 'Sure.

Thanks, Katy. Now you trot off and be about your business. *Outside*, though.'

'Hey,' she said. 'What about my two dollars?'

'Put it down to expenses.'

The two detectives turned now to face Henry Mortimer, and all traces of the bantering tone in which they had earlier spoken to him were gone.

'All right, Henry,' said O'Connor.

'The full story,' said Nugent.

'And don't leave anything out.'

'But . . . I — I could lose my job if this gets out.'

'That's right, Henry.'

'If I tell you — '

'Yes?'

'Will you promise — ?'

'Promise, Henry?'

'Yes, not to tell — not to mention it here. If my mother — '

'Ah, now he's going to tell us how it would break his mother's heart that he hustles whores for ground rights in the hotel lobby,' Nugent said.

'Gets you right here,' O'Connor said.

'Talk, Henry,' suggested Nugent.

Henry talked. He had a sort of loose working arrangement with the girls who patrolled Broadway and the adjoining corners around the hotel. When things were quiet on the street, or if the weather turned foul, they could stroll around the lobby of the hotel for ten minutes. That was the deal. Ten minutes and no more. For this privilege they paid him $2 per week in advance. If they hooked a John they had to arrange to take him elsewhere. That was also part of the deal, and most of the girls were happy to play along. After all, your chances of hooking a John in the lobby of the Grand Central were sufficiently improved to make it well worth $2, and in the kind of time allowed to them there was no way they could draw themselves to the attention of the house detective without being very, very stupid. Henry assured the detectives that he screened the girls very carefully to make sure none of the ones who might cause a scene and cost him his livelihood were never allowed in.

'You can understand, can't you?' he pleaded. 'I was really very discreet.'

'We'll bet you were,' Nugent said. 'Now tell us about Lily Purcell.'

'Lily Purcell?'

'Lily Purcell.' Nugent pushed the photograph in front of the clerk.

'This Lily Purcell. The one who was murdered.'

Mortimer shuddered.

'What about her?' he said.

'Did you see her recently, Henry?'

'I — I can't recall.'

'How about last Thursday, Henry?'

'Thursday?'

'The twentieth.'

'At about ten-thirty, or afterwards.'

'No,' Mortimer said. 'I don't think so.'

'But you're not sure.'

'No.'

'You'd remember if you had?'

'I think so.'

'Did she come in here much?'

'Now and then.'

'How often is that, Henry?'

'Once, twice a week, perhaps. No more. I wouldn't let any of them in more often than that, in case anyone got to know them, realize what they were doing.'

'When was she in here last?'

'I can't remember.'

'Try.'

'Last Tuesday, or maybe it was Monday. I can't be sure.'

'You were sure of getting their money, though.'

'Well . . .'

'What time last Tuesday, or Monday?'

'I don't . . . It was Tuesday. About nine-thirty. I remember because there weren't many people around when she came in.'

'What was she wearing?'

'A black cloak, I think. No hat. A scarf, that's it. Red flowers on it.'

'Did she connect?'

'What?'

'Connect, Henry,' Nugent explained patiently. 'Find a mark, a John. Did she pick anyone up?'

'Uh. I — I don't know.'

'Henry, we could always continue this very interesting discussion over at Mulberry Street, if you'd prefer.'

'Oh, no. God, no, you wouldn't — ?'

'Want to bet, Henry?'

'Bastards!' Mortimer hissed. Nugent looked at O'Connor, who shrugged.

'Henry,' O'Connor said, his voice soft and reproachful. He leaned forward into the corner, and Nugent crowded quite close to his left so that people in the lobby could not see too clearly what was happening. What was happening was that O'Connor's huge paw had taken Henry Mortimer by the part of his shirt where the tie is knotted, the collar, bow-tie and upper part of Mortimer's waistcoat screwed up in the detective's iron grasp, and was lifting Henry Mortimer up on his toes like some kind of amateur ballet dancer. Henry Mortimer's face, his breathing cut off by this treatment, went a dull, suffused red. His eyes bulged and his hands made flapping movements. O'Connor let him down with a bump and Mortimer slumped against the wall, his

114

breathing ragged.

'Now then,' said O'Connor reasonably.

Mortimer nodded. He knew when he was licked, and he didn't like the look in O'Connor's narrowed eyes or relish the thought of a second helping of the treatment he had just received.

'She picked someone up,' Nugent supplied. 'A guest?'

Mortimer nodded. 'Yes.'

'Name?'

'Sylvester Henderson,' Mortimer said. 'Room 551.'

'What time?'

'Nine-forty, nine-forty-five.'

'He went out with her?'

'Yes.'

'But she didn't come in here on Thursday the twentieth?'

'No.'

'You're sure, Henry?'

Henry Mortimer nodded again. All he wanted now was to be left alone. The big man had hurt him. He'd have bruises on his throat, and Mother would want to know how he'd got them.

'Okay,' O'Connor said. 'You want to

check him out, Andy? After all, it's your case.'

'Sure,' Nugent said.

'I'll get on over to Second,' O'Connor said. 'Want to take another crack at finding someone who saw that girl.'

'The trunk thing, you mean?'

'Uhuh.'

'Getting anywhere?'

'Nope.'

'Me neither,' said Nugent. 'See you later.'

★   ★   ★

Joe Petrosino wasn't getting anywhere either, which was why he asked to see the Chief.

Everyone in the Detective Corps called Inspector Thomas F. Byrnes the Chief. Somehow it seemed the only way to describe him, although from time to time it confused visitors, who assumed that the Chief being referred to must be the Chief of Police. In actual fact the Detective Corps had a name for the Chief of Police, too, but they weren't allowed to say it aloud within the environs of Headquarters.

Inspector Byrnes had an office on the first floor of the six-storey building whose official address was 200 Mulberry Street. The fact that the building took up an entire city block and was full of rambling stairwells and cubby-hole offices that had been known to create a sense of loss of direction in new recruits to the force was often overlooked, as was the fact that the building was very strategically located in almost the exact geographical centre of the heart of Manhattan, fourteen blocks south of Union Square and fifteen north of City Hall.

The office that Joe Petrosino was now in was a tall, sunny room with a big window that looked out on the bustle of Houston Street. It contained a huge desk, bookcases lining one wall, an old metal safe, several brass cuspidors, a glass-fronted cabinet containing Byrnes's collection of old pistols and a smaller table near the door littered with papers. The walls were covered with framed certificates, some photographs and an old painting of some yachts rounding Sandy Hook lighthouse.

Inspector Byrnes was Irish.

Born in Loughrea, County Galway, he had come to America in the second year of the Civil War and as soon as he was old enough he had joined the police force. He had risen rapidly through the ranks: patrolman, roundsman, sergeant, captain. In 1878 had become an inspector. Behind him, in every precinct he had worked in — and there had been many, because an honest copper tended to get moved on when the various fixes and pay-offs being operated on the streets were threatened by his presence — he had left behind the reputation of being an 'unfixable' cop. To understand just what this means it is necessary to realize that there were all sorts of perks in the ordinary way of being a cop that very few ever questioned. Your friendly cop on the beat would obviously look after your interests a little better if you were 'friendly'. So you could pay him some kind of tribute, a way of saying 'thank you', no more. If he was a drinking man you could see to it that he never went short of something: a bottle of good wine, maybe, or even just a cold beer every day when he came by in the summer. If he had a family, you could slip him one of your good pieces of meat, undercharging badly and writing the difference down to good relations with the police. If you were a crook, of course, you could simply slip him a few dollars a week not to crack down on your policy bank, your keno layout, your unlicensed grog shop, or whatever. If you were unlucky enough to get arrested you could even talk some of them out of going through with it. Ready money talked a language many, many cops understood quite well. There were plenty of men on the payroll of the Tweed Ring who could get anything fixed, because there were always plenty of cops who owed them a favour. But Byrnes was not one of them and never had been. In consequence of which he was feared or respected in direct relation to where your sympathies lay. In simple terms any crook, dodger, ward-heeler or fixer who tried to bend, circumambulate or break the law on a fairly regular basis hated and loathed Thomas Byrnes, whereas every man on the Detective Corps admired and respected him. He never snowed them, never lied to them, never played favourites among them. He was what they called a 'book' man. He played everything by the rules, by the book. If you did the same, you could write your own ticket. If you didn't, God help you.

He was a big man, Tom Byrnes, almost six feet tall, broad-shouldered and burly, with a heavy moustache already sprinkled with grey. His eyes were a bright, inquisitive blue, and his hands were gnarled and massive, the hands of a street fighter. He had an instinctive understanding of the patient, plodding, unexciting work of the detective, and knew that no conviction ever comes from sloppy, hasty inquiry. He had hand-picked every man on his Detective Corps himself. And he was proud of every one of them.

'Something wrong, Joe?' he asked.

'Something I can't put my finger on, sir,' Petrosino said, taking the chair that Byrnes waved towards. He sat down heavily. His feet hurt like hell. The sooner they built that Rapid Transit System they were always talking about the better it would be. You could cover a lot of ground on foot in a day's work, and Petrosino was covering more than usual right now.

'Tell me,' Byrnes said. He leaned back in his creaky bentwood armchair and lit a black cigar. It smelled like someone cooking old horse manure. Byrnes inhaled the smoke with every indication of enjoyment as Petrosino outlined the events he had been investigating, the mysterious explosion at the bakery, the old shoe-repairer with the now-useless hand, and his total inability to get any kind of information off the street.

'Clannish as hell, down there,' Byrnes said. 'Always were.'

'I agree, sir,' Petrosino said, 'but this is not normal. I mean, not with me. I can usually talk to anyone down there, get information. Instead they're all as tight as clams.'

'Know why?'

'A guess, anyway,' Petrosino said.

Slowly, taking his time and choosing his

words carefully so that it wouldn't come out sounding like something in the *Police Gazette*, Petrosino told the Inspector what his father had told him about the Italian 'men of respect', the growth of their power, and finally his feeling that perhaps it was spreading to the United States. Byrnes listened in silence, and when Petrosino had finished he asked a question.

'I want to see if I can join them,' Petrosino said. 'If there is such a thing as the Mafia, I want to find out where it is, and see if I can get on the inside of it.'

'How?'

'I'd need a special authority from you, sir, taking me off normal duties. Then I could start looking for work, down at the docks, maybe, or in one of the restaurants in Little Italy.'

'Have you got any idea how short-staffed I am, Joe?' Byrnes said.

'Yes, sir,' Petrosino replied meekly. There wasn't a detective on the Corps handling less than six cases at any one time, often many more.

'And you want me to take you out of

circulation completely for — how long?'

'At least two months, sir,' Petrosino said, thinking 'in for a penny . . .'.

Byrnes frowned. He got up from his chair and went across to the big window, looking down at the street without really seeing anything. After a few minutes he turned round.

'Let me be sure I've got this straight,' Byrnes said. 'You feel — you haven't any evidence, but you *feel* — that there's some kind of secret society down in Little Italy, working what *could* be an extortion racket on the shopkeepers and business-men. You don't know who, *if anyone*, is behind it, or whether it is or is not called — what was it again?'

'The Mafia, sir.'

'Mafia, yes. What a name! Well, then, whether it's this Mafia your father knows about from the old days or not, your reasons for believing that it *may* be are that the local people *seem* to be frightened to the extent that they will not talk to anyone about what's happening. Is that about right?'

'Yes, sir,' Petrosino said, sheepishly. Put

123

like that it did sound like something out of the *Police Gazette*.

'When do you want to start?' Byrnes asked, taking Petrosino completely by surprise.

'Right away, if it can be arranged,' he replied quickly.

'What's your case book like?'

'Nothing really heavy, sir. I've been concentrating on this business.'

'Hand over everything you're working on to Charlie Heidelberg,' Byrnes said. 'You'll need a contact if you're going under cover.'

'No, sir,' Petrosino said. 'I want to go entirely alone. If what my old man tells me is true, these people are everywhere. I want it so the only people who know where I am are yourself and me. For the record, I'll be on leave, gone out West somewhere with, say, suspected consumption — except that it won't be true.'

'I could arrange that, I suppose,' Byrnes mused. 'But aren't you putting an awful lot of weight into this, Joe? We've got enough on our hands, God knows, without Italian secret societies.'

'Inspector,' Petrosino said. 'If I'm wrong, all you'll have lost will be a little time. I'll make that up by working twice as hard afterwards. But if I'm right . . . '

'Point taken,' Byrnes said. It was one of his favourite sayings.

'Then I can start?'

'I thought I already said that,' growled Byrnes. 'Get on with it, Joe. I haven't got all day to sit chewing the fat with you!'

Petrosino grinned and went out of the office. Sergeant Isaac Bird, sitting in his usual place outside the Inspector's door, looked up incuriously. Petrosino took a breath and decided to get started.

'Damn, damn, damn,' he said softly.

'What's up, Joe?' Bird asked, sympathetically. Petrosino wasn't the first detective to come out of that door and say those words.

'I got to put in for sick leave,' Petrosino said petulantly. 'Some damn flummery about suspected consumption. Load of horse turds!'

'Sure,' Bird said, but Petrosino had already noticed the slight recoil, the vague shrinking-away, that retreat from the unknown that was the usual reaction to the presence of anyone with lung sickness.

'That's tough, Joe,' Bird said.

'Yeah,' Petrosino said, scowling. Then he pretended to brighten, and slapped Bird on the back. 'What the hell,' he said, as if forcing cheerfulness. 'They tell me Santa Fé is right pretty.'

'That where you're going?'

'I'm told that's one of the best places,' Petrosino said.

'Good luck, then,' Bird told him. 'Let's know if you strike gold.'

6

Alfred Johnson was very, very angry.

He was, first of all, angry with himself for having been a complete and utter twenty-four-carat idiot. Naturally, he could not be expected to go on thinking of himself in those terms, and it was not long before he transferred his anger to the city of New York and in particular the island of Manhattan, a teeming, filthy, hostile and uncivilized place where a decent, respectable, hard-working British businessman could be accosted in the busy streets at high noon (or thereabouts, he thought, let's not be finicky about this), accosted, he said, by patent rogues, outright swindlers, conscienceless thieves, cut-purses, highwaymen, robbers — probably armed, there was no way he could be certain that they had not been. After venting his rage for a while upon the heads of Colonel Robert E. Lee Devereaux and his accomplice, the seaman Blundy, Johnson's ire naturally now turned to the people whose laziness, importunity, slipshodness and lackadaisical interest in the safety and welfare not only of their own people but (even more important) of decent, respectable businessmen who made long, expensive and arduous journeys in search of trade to this stinking, polluted Gomorrah. In other words, the police. The more he thought about it, the more he became sure that if it had not been for the laxity of the police Devereaux and his stooge could hardly have operated on the sidewalk of a thoroughfare well known for its traffic in visiting businessmen from abroad.

So Alfred Johnson determined to take his case directly to the Chief of Police of the City of New York. By the time he had been gently shunted from there to the desk sergeant, who took down the details of the outrage as if it was nothing more interesting than the result of a horse race upon which he hadn't bet, and from there to the waiting room and from there to the desk in the Detective Corps premises and, finally, to Ed Slevin, Alfred Johnson was, as they say, spitting buttons. He sat fuming as Slevin carefully read the details that the desk sergeant had taken down. He controlled his mounting temper as Slevin appeared to spend some time reading documents patently pertaining to something totally different. He finally exploded when Slevin walked across the room and came back carrying a huge black leather book, which he put down on the desk in front of Johnson.

'Young man!' said Johnson, breathing heavily. 'How much longer am I to be kept waiting?'

Slevin looked up, surprised. He was only just over regulation height, about five feet nine, very slim, fair-haired, boyish-looking. He seemed on first impression to be young, and you had to look closer to see the tired lines of experience round the eyes, and in the set of the mouth. Ed Slevin was thirty. He looked about twenty-two.

'I'm sorry, sir,' he said. 'I wasn't keeping you waiting, I was getting the K O book.' Seeing Johnson's befuddled expression, he explained, 'K O means Known Offenders,' he said. 'We have descriptions, sometimes even photographs, of various kinds of criminals on file here. This book is the bunco boys.'

'The what?'

'Bunco,' Slevin explained. 'Fleecers, fakers, bunco-steerers, con artists, hype merchants.' The blank look on Johnson's face persisted. 'Confidence tricksters,' Slevin tried, glad to see Johnson's furrowed brow clear. He slid the book nearer to the Englishman, who looked at it aghast.

'Do you mean to tell me that you have a book *full* of these people, and that you know who they are?'

'Why, yes, sir.' Slevin said, puzzled.

'Then why aren't they in jail where they belong, instead of on the streets robbing innocent people?' snapped Johnson.

'I'm afraid we can't just go out and lock them up because they are known to us, sir,' Slevin said. 'They have to be arrested because of, or in the commission of, a crime.'

'But if you know that their profession is

that of a criminal,' Johnson said, 'surely you don't just leave them free to roam the streets?'

'Sir,' Slevin said, tiredly. 'Would you be kind enough to look through the book and see if there is anyone in there who looks or sounds like the man you claim robbed you?'

'Claim?' said Johnson. 'I assure you that I most certainly do not claim any such thing, young man. I assert it, I aver it, I swear it, I guarantee it, I state it as an incontrovertible fact, but I do not *claim* it.'

'Yes, sir,' Slevin said. He was pretty tired, and a hysterical Englishman who had paid the price of his own greed by falling for the diamond-switching routine which, apart from anything else, was one of the oldest confidence tricks in the business wasn't exactly the happy ending to his day that he would have wished. However, he was a public servant, and so he kept his peace and turned the pages for Johnson.

'We have no record of any known bunco man using the name Devereaux,' he told Johnson. 'So let's concentrate on the details. You say,' he referred to the form filled in by the desk sergeant, 'he was between fifty and sixty, distinguished-looking, grey-haired, tall. How tall was he?'

'Oh, I don't know,' Johnson said. 'Six feet?'

'How tall are you, sir?'

'Five feet nine.'

'So he was taller than you?'

'Yes. No, wait a minute. No, he wasn't. Well, maybe a little. But not much.'

'Say five feet ten inches, then,' Slevin said, making a note on the form. 'Grey suit, grey hat. Colour of eyes not known. Colonel Robert E. Lee Devereaux.'

Any American being given a name like that would have run for the nearest cop, he thought. Goddammit, it even *sounded* phoney!

'All the five feet tens are in this section,' he explained. 'We cross-reference them by height, weight, hair and eye colour and so on. Look through all these carefully, and see if any of them looks like the man you met.'

He went back round his desk as Johnson leafed slowly through the book. A reliable guess, he thought, would be that thirty, forty or fifty people a day were bamboozled out of money, jewellery or precious possessions by bunco men. They came in all the time. Sometimes it would be an immigrant who had stopped to stare at the soaring piers of the new bridge which was being built across the East River to Brooklyn. Someone would sidle up to him, remark upon the wonders of modern science. If the mark took the bait he might very well end up discovering that the person he was talking to was the actual owner of the new bridge, which would one day be worth millions and millions. Unfortunately the owner was faced with terrible problems of keeping on with the work. A loss on the Stock Exchange, perhaps, or a fire that had burned down his home, wiping out his family and his will to continue. The variations were endless, the result always the same. He was prepared to sell the bridge for any reasonable sum. And someone, sooner or later, fell for it. The gullibility of people was endless, not to mention awesome. He'd seen them all: people who'd bought Cunarders lying at anchor in the North River, people who'd bought the Astor House or the A. T. Stewart store, often poor people who had brought all their savings from the Old Country to the New and were left penniless and destitute by the predators who had seen them coming and stripped them as mercilessly as if they had been dying lambs and the bunco-steerers vultures. The old diamond-switch routine, for which Johnson had fallen, was a real standby, its origins lost somewhere in the mists of antiquity, the land of Nod to which Cain was banished most likely, Slevin thought. He often had the feeling that all the crooks in the world had their origins in the land of Nod. It had always sounded that kind of place when his mother had read it out from the family bible.

'This one looks a bit like him,' he heard Johnson say.

He came round the desk and looked at the picture at which the Englishman was pointing. The photograph was not that of a distinguished-looking southern colonel. It was a head-and-shoulders picture of a man of perhaps forty, stern-faced and upright in appearance. On the bottom right-hand corner was written B742 in Indian ink. 'B742' Slevin nodded, and went across the room to a series of wooden filing cabinets. In these were stored the dossiers that Byrnes's staff had laboriously compiled from existing fragments and records and their own arrests. One of the first things Byrne had done was to institute a requirement that any detective making an arrest likely to result in a conviction should attempt, if it was possible, to obtain a photograph of the criminal, from either his place of abode, his family, or any other place where one might be found. This was then placed with what Byrnes called the *modus operandi* document, a written report by the arresting officer that outlined the criminal's activities, reasons for arrest, place where arrested, sentence given, present whereabouts where known, last place of residence, physical description and names (where known) of any accomplices with whom he regularly worked. Byrnes had started this system on the principle that the majority of criminals were fools who would rather cheat, steal or kill than work. The majority of them, both in America and elsewhere, seemed to have special lines of work to which they always returned. Knock off a burglar working in the midtown area and send him up for six months. As soon as he came out he'd be back burgling in the midtown area again. Arrest a drunk in the vilest grog shop in Five Points and put him in the pokey overnight. The next night you'd have to do it all over again: same offence, same locale, sometimes even round the same time of day or night.

Byrnes's theory was a rough-and-ready one, but it worked. That is to say, it worked in so far as the file was light years away from being comprehensive in a city that boasted anything up to two hundred arrests every day of the year. But it was a damned sight better than nothing, and a hell of a sight better than anything that the Detective Corps of New York had ever had to work with before.

'Well?' asked Johnson.

'This could be your man,' Slevin said, guardedly. 'He's about the right age, and he'll have changed some since the photo was taken.'

'Well, then,' Johnson said. 'Why don't you go out and arrest him?'

'I'm afraid it's not that easy, sir.'

'What.'

'You see, Mr Johnson,' Slevin explained patiently. 'The transaction you were involved in took place on the street. There were no witnesses. It's only your word against his.'

'My word is not in question, young man,' Johnson said. 'Surely it is worth more than the word of a known criminal?'

'Of course, sir,' Slevin said, tactfully. 'But without a witness . . . '

'The jeweller!' Johnson snapped triumphantly.

'Yes, sir,' Slevin said. 'What was the name of the jeweller?'

'What?'

'The name of the jeweller who appraised the diamonds.'

'Name? I don't know the man's name,' Johnson said.

'Can you remember the address, sir?'

'Address. Yes. Well — not, actually. I mean, it was on Broadway. Down below City Hall. I remember that.'

'There are over two thousand jewellery stores in Manhattan, Mr Johnson,' Slevin said. 'Can you be a little more specific?'

'Well,' Johnson said. 'We walked across to Broadway from Cortlandt. Then we turned left up Broadway.'

'One block? Two? Three?'

'Two or three, I can't be sure.'

'I see,' sighed Slevin. 'Could you find the store again if I sent a patrolman over there with you?'

'I think so,' Johnson said. 'Although I can't be sure. What has all this to do with arresting Bateman?'

'Well, sir, if the jeweller remembers you coming in with Bateman, we can at least establish that he did indeed have diamonds, that he also knows you, which gives us both opportunity and presence, which are important in trying to establish fraud.'

'But I've already told you that.'

'Yes, sir, but that isn't proof acceptable in a court.'

'What do I have to do, get robbed in plain view of a policeman?'

'If you have to get robbed at all, sir, that would be useful.'

'Don't you give me any cheek, young man,' Johnson snapped. 'I have some influential friends in this city. I will not tolerate disrespect from the police or anyone else. I have been robbed and I demand that you arrest the man responsible.'

'Yes, sir,' Slevin said. Funny how they all had influential friends, he thought. He'd long since lost count of the number of times he'd been told that he'd lose his job if he didn't mind his tongue.

'Well?' Johnson demanded.

'I'll get a patrolman to go across to Broadway with you, sir,' Slevin said. 'If you can find the jeweller, and if he's prepared to swear that Bateman is the man who came into the store with you, then I can take steps to bring Bateman in for questioning. Otherwise, I'm afraid there's little we can do.'

'This simply isn't good enough,' Johnson said. 'I demand to see your superior officer.'

'I'm sorry, Mr Johnson,' Slevin said. 'The Inspector doesn't get involved in routine investigations.'

'Are you telling me I cannot see the Inspector?' Johnson asked ominously, rising from his chair.

'No, sir, I'm suggesting that I can handle this matter perfectly well,' Slevin recited. 'If you'll allow me to continue.'

Johnson sat down.

'I just want my money back,' he said. 'I really can't afford to lose that much money, you know.'

'I know, sir,' Slevin said.

'Well,' Johnson said, realizing that for a moment he had let slip the mask of power and wealth he had (unsuccessfully, but he didn't know that) been trying to project. 'Where's that patrolman, eh?'

'If you'll wait here a moment, sir,'

Slevin said. 'I'll send someone down-stairs.'

'Be as quick as you can, will you?' Johnson said. 'I'm a busy man, you know.'

Slevin nodded and went across to the desk sergeant. If he was mentally comparing his work load of something like twenty or thirty pending cases, six live ones, two dozen reports still to be written, the fact that he had had only eighteen hours sleep in the last five days, and in the same period only three good meals, his face showed no sign of it. All the same, he damned to eternal hell all gullible fools, especially gullible English fools, damned them to the permanent hell of spending eternity being conned out of their money, their clothes, their homes, their carriages, their family fortunes, their possessions and their insufferable middle-class righteousness.

Then he shook his head wryly, reflecting that if such a hell ever came to pass, odds were he'd be the detective assigned to it.

★ ★ ★

'Hello, dearie,' Sarah Dawkins smiled. 'Lookin' for a good time?'

The man in the dark suit stopped, half turning to look closely at her. Sarah was a bold little thing and no mistake. Her face was saucy, her eyes wide and mischievous-looking. She had on a tight-fitting calico dress with a bodice that was cut quite low, revealing the swell of her breasts. She was nearly thirty, old for the game, but as long as the light wasn't too direct she looked quite attractive, what common people referred to as 'cute'.

'What's your name?' the man asked her. He had a deep voice and his eyes were dark pools of blackness under the flaring gas lamp on the corner of Spring Street and Broadway.

'Sarah,' she simpered. 'What's yours?'

'Niemand,' he said. His long, supple fingers toyed with the heavy gold watch-chain looped across the front of his waistcoat. Sarah noticed the movement and her heart jumped a bit at the sight of the chain. Solid gold, that, she told herself. Sarah, me girl, this is a fat one.

She pasted her most winning smile on her face.

'You come with me, dearie,' she said, laying a hand on his arm. 'I'll make you feel good.'

'Will you?' he said softly. The question made Sarah frown for a moment, but she shrugged off the faint feeling of mistrust that touched her thoughts for a second. He ought to be good for $10 if she looked after him all right.

'What's your other name, darlin'?' she asked.

'Niemand will do,' he said. 'Have you got a room?'

'No,' she said, 'but we could go to a place I know. It's quite ch — it's not expensive.' She leaned against him, and let her hand artlessly touch him. He was ready for it, she thought. 'Or would you rather . . . ?'

She jerked her head towards the darker street behind them.

'Yes,' he said. He was breathing shallowly and Sarah smiled to herself.

'That'll be ten dollars then, darlin',' she said.

'Yes,' he said again. He put a note into her hand and started to walk towards the darkness of Spring Street.

Sarah held up the note to the light. It was a ten-spot, all right. She looked across Broadway at the brightly lit, block-long frontage of the St Nicholas Hotel. She'd seen ever such a ducky little shawl in the window of Genin's Bazaar, one of the shops attached to the hotel. Tomorrow she'd go in there and buy it, enjoying the looks on the faces of the stuck-up shopgirls who would have to serve her, knowing how she got her money, knowing that it would take them two months to save enough to buy such a pretty nonsense.

'Come on, then, dearie,' she said, taking Niemand's hand. They walked perhaps twenty yards along Spring to where there was a narrow alley running between two business houses. There was a doorway at the back of one of them that Sarah found useful for her purposes. It was in complete shadow and when you stood in the doorway you could no more be seen from the street

144

than if you were on the moon.

'Here we are,' she said. 'This is nice, isn't it?'

'Yes,' he said. He touched her face in the darkness, and she lifted her head, oddly moved by what she thought was a gesture of tenderness. In fact the man was simply establishing where her throat was and as Sarah's chin touched his left hand the man clamped her in a terrible, strangling grip as the other hand with the razor in it moved in wicked, ruining movements up and across her arching body.

7

Sylvester Henderson was fat.

Not the beefy, athlete-run-to-seed-fat kind of fat, but gross, the bulging, wobbling, unhealthy-wheezing-fat kind of fat. Andy Nugent guessed the man's weight at about 260 pounds and thought him a fairly repulsive specimen. But of course, looks weren't everything. Maybe his mother loved him.

He showed Henderson his copper shield (it never occurred to him any more that it was because he carried it that he was called a copper) and Henderson frowned.

'Police?' he said, in a high, thin, nervous voice. 'What is it?'

'Detective Nugent,' Nugent said. 'Like to ask you a couple of questions, Mr Henderson.'

'About what?'

'Couldn't we talk inside, sir?'

'First you tell me what this is about, officer.'

146

'Murder,' Nugent said flatly.

'Come inside,' Henderson replied.

He had a sitting-room and bedroom to himself. As far as Nugent could see there was no sign of a regular female occupant. At $20 a day Henderson obviously wasn't short of money.

'You here alone, sir?' he asked.

'Yes, yes,' Henderson said impatiently. 'Now what's all this about a murder?'

'Do you know a woman named Lily Purcell?'

'Purcell? Purcell? No, can't say I do. She in business in town, or what?'

'She used to be in business, Mr Henderson. She's dead.'

'Oh, I see. That's the murder you spoke of.'

'That's it.'

'Well, I can't help you. I never heard of her.'

'Sure of that, Mr Henderson?'

The fat man frowned. 'Are you doubting my word?'

'Mr Henderson,' Nugent said patiently, 'we have a witness prepared to swear that he saw you talking with Lily Purcell on

147

Tuesday last — that's the eighteenth — in the lobby downstairs, and that you left the hotel with her.'

Sylvester Henderson's face went white, and he sat down rather suddenly in a chair by the paper-strewn table. Nugent winced as the floor trembled at the impact, half expecting the chair to break apart. It held, and Sylvester Henderson reached into his pocket and withdrew a large handkerchief, mopping a broad brow which was suddenly wet with perspiration.

'Oh,' he said. 'Ah.'

'You don't deny you met Purcell downstairs and went out with her?'

'Uh,' said Sylvester Henderson.

'And then?'

'Ah?'

'And then? Did you have intercourse with her?'

'Ulp,' said Henderson. 'Excuse me,' he added, and went out of the room fast into the bedroom. Nugent went swiftly after him, but Henderson was only running some water into a glass at the washstand in the corner of the room. Henderson gulped the water down and then sat heavily on the edge of the bed. Nugent winced again, but everything held.

'Well, Mr Henderson?' he asked.

'I . . . uh . . . I didn't know her name,' Henderson said. He was panting as if he had run up a flight of stairs. 'Didn't know her name.' He looked up at Nugent as if he were about to say a prayer. 'Will it be in the newspapers?' he asked.

'Not unless you talk to a newspaperman, Mr Henderson,' Nugent said.

'It's the wife, you see,' Henderson babbled. 'She's, you know, delicate. Anaemia, the doctors say. She doesn't . . . she — '

'No need to tell me any of this, Mr Henderson,' Nugent said roughly.

'No, no, so you'll appreciate my — so you'll understand why. Why I. Why I went with. That woman.'

'You knew she was a prostitute?'

'Yes. Yes. The clerk told me.'

'The desk clerk? Henry Mortimer?'

'Henry. Yes. Henry. I spoke with her. No names, you see. I didn't know her name.'

'Where did you go with her?'

'Wh — where?'

'Yes, where?'

'An alley. Not far. Around the corner of Broadway.'

Nugent nodded. It figured Lily had used the place regularly. Had the killer known that? With robbery, rivalry and 'family' removed as motives (that is to say murder committed by someone related to or intimately close to the victim, which is the largest percentile area of all murder) he was at a loss. He had talked to everyone on the street who might have seen the girl prior to her death. So far the only lead he'd come up with was this frightened fat man.

'Did you see her again after the Tuesday?'

'Well, no.'

'How do you mean?'

'I never went with her again.'

'But you saw her again?'

'Listen, Mr — ?'

'Nugent.'

'Listen, Mr Nugent,' Henderson said, anxiously. 'I'm a respectable married man.

I've got a little dry-goods wholesaling business down in Allentown, Pennsylvania. If this got out, it could ruin me.'

'Mr Henderson,' Nugent said levelly, 'I am investigating a vicious murder. My first duty is to find the person or persons who killed Lily Purcell. If I can keep your name out of it, I will. But you've got to tell me everything you know.'

'It's my wife, you see,' Henderson said. 'She's — '

'Delicate, I know. Now, did you see the Purcell woman again after the Tuesday?'

'I saw her. Yes. On the street, you understand. I didn't talk to her.'

'When was this, exactly?'

'About eleven, I suppose. On the Thursday night.'

'The twentieth?'

'That's right.'

'Was she alone?'

'Well, she was at first.'

'At first?'

'I was coming down Broadway, you see. I went to the St Denis to meet some people. Business, you know. We had dinner. I stopped in a saloon on the way down for a few drinks. Then I walked back to the hotel. I could see her standing on the corner.'

'Which corner?'

'The corner of Third and Broadway.'

'But you didn't speak to her.'

'No,' Henderson said. 'She was talking to someone. A man.'

'A man? Can you describe what he looked like?'

'Well,' Henderson said. 'It was pretty late. Dark there. I'd had a couple of drinks.'

'Try, Mr Henderson,' Nugent urged him. 'It's very important.'

'Well, you see, to tell the truth, I was half thinking I might well . . . you know . . . I might. I'd had a few drinks, you see.'

'But when you got there she was talking to a man.'

'That's right. Big fellow, husky built.' There was a thin edge of envy in his voice and Nugent could picture how he might have felt. Coming down Broadway with a bellyful of good food and some drinks to get his blood moving, toying with the idea of a tumble with a whore to round off a pleasant evening away from hearth and home, only to find his rosy plan spoiled by a big husky fellow.

'What happened then?'

'I thought I'd wait awhile, in case . . . '

'In case he went away?'

'Yes. You know, not watching them, exactly. Just waiting to see.'

'What happened?

'They talked for a few minutes. Then they went off down Third Street together.'

'What did you do then?'

'I came back to the hotel and went to bed.'

'And that's all?'

'Yes, I swear it.'

'All right, Mr Henderson. Let's get back to this man Purcell was talking to. He was big, you say. Husky?'

'That's right. Not as big as you, though.'

'How tall would you say?'

'How tall are you?'

'Six feet, even.'

'Then he'd have been around five ten, something like that.'

'What was he wearing?'

'Dark clothes. I really didn't see him all that clearly.'

'How long did you wait while he talked to the woman?'

'Oh, five minutes. Not more.'

'You stood watching them for five minutes and you can't remember anything more than that? Where were you?'

'On the — see here, I don't like your tone.'

'I'm not mad about it myself. Where were you?'

'On — on the opposite corner.'

'Across Broadway?'

'No. No, the same side.'

Nugent sighed. Henderson had been standing not more than thirty yards away from the probable killer of Lily Purcell, and he was being coy about it because he didn't want anyone to think he was a peeping Tom.

'Let's try it another way,' Nugent said. 'First, was he wearing an overcoat?'

'No. No, he wasn't.'

'A suit.'

'Yes. A blue suit.'

'Blue? Good. Carrying anything? A parcel, box, satchel, case?'

'No. Nothing I could see.'

'A young man?'

'No, I don't think so. He didn't walk like a young man.'

'But not old?'

'You mean really old? No, not elderly.'

'Forty? Fifty?'

'Nearer forty than fifty, if you want my guess.'

'How old are you, Mr Henderson?'

'Forty-four.'

'And how old would you say I was?'

'Thirty-ish. Thirty-three, -four, maybe?'

'Actually, I'm not quite thirty,' Nugent grinned. 'But I've had a lot of worries.'

'I beg your pardon?'

'Nothing,' Nugent said. 'Let's run over this again. The man you saw was about five feet ten, husky, wearing a blue suit, aged around forty to forty-five. Is that right?'

'That's right.'

'Can you remember anything else about him? Anything at all, no matter how small?'

Henderson frowned. 'No,' he said after a moment. 'Except the watch-chain.'

'What about the watch-chain?'

'I could see it shining in the street lights,' Henderson said. 'A heavy gold watch-chain.'

'Did it have a seal, anything like that?'

'I really couldn't say, Mr Nugent,' Henderson said. 'I really couldn't.'

'Very well,' the detective said. 'And then they went off together down Third Street?'

'That's right.'

'While you came back here and went to bed.'

'Right.'

'You didn't stick around to see if Lily would come back, maybe?'

'No, I didn't.'

'And you didn't decide to find yourself another girl.'

'Mr Nugent, I've already told you what I did. Your questions are becoming offensive.' Henderson, now that the thing was off his mind, was getting some of his steam back. Andy Nugent grinned to himself.

'Here's my card,' he said, handing Henderson a slip of pasteboard. 'If you'd just come down to Headquarters tomorrow and make a statement and sign it?'

'I can't do that,' Henderson said, the pomposity deserting him like air let out of a balloon. 'I've got to be back in Allentown tomorrow night.'

'Send a telegram,' Nugent suggested. 'Tell your wife you've been delayed. Tell her anything you like. But don't leave town until you check with us. If you'd be so kind,' he added.

'But, I, this is — this is outrageous,' spluttered Henderson. 'You have no right to detain me here. Have you any idea what these rooms cost per day?'

'I didn't say you have to stay here, sir,' Nugent said. 'I asked you not to leave town without checking with Headquarters. You come by tomorrow and make your statement, and odds are you'll be on your way back to Allentown an hour later.'

'I shall speak to your superior officer about this,' Henderson said.

'You do that, Mr Henderson,' Nugent said, wearily. 'Tomorrow.'

Frank O'Connor played a hunch.

It was a cinch that if you were a young girl in trouble there were a set of severely limited choices open to you.

You could, of course, go to the man who was the father-to-be, and ask him, or beg him (depending upon the relationship) to give your child a name and save you from scandal and disgrace. Providing he wasn't already married, of course. Providing he wasn't wealthy, so that his parents would refuse to allow their son to ruin his career, his future prospects, his entire life by admitting the paternity of a child by some common creature whose morals — obviously — were no better than those of a, well, one of those women.

Let's suppose Mary didn't have that option, he thought. (He called her Mary, simply to give the dead woman some kind of personality, a real existence prior to the time she had entered his own life as a corpse, a nameless, faceless, dead thing.)

The next option was to have the babe.

Well, no need to go into that. The final course was to have an abortion.

There was just one problem. It was not only against the law to have an abortion, but it was against the law to procure one. The New York State laws were adamant upon the subject: 'The wilful killing of an unborn quick child by any injury to the mother of the child, which would be murder if it resulted in the death of such mother, shall be deemed manslaughter in the first degree.' Which meant, for the mother-to-be, a term of not less than seven years in the pokey, the penitentiary, if she got herself an abortion. The law was no less tough on the abortionist:

Every person who shall administer to any woman pregnant with a quick child, or prescribe for any such woman, or advise and procure for any such woman, any medicine, drugs or substance whatever, or shall use and employ any instrument or other means, with intent thereby to destroy such child, unless the same shall have been necessary to save the life of such mother shall, in the case of death of such child or such mother thereby produced, be deemed guilty of man-slaughter in the second degree.

Prison sentence four to seven years.

Which made a man wonder how come there were advertisements in every newspaper, in every magazine, in shop windows, cigar stores, and news-stands offering 'Sure Cures for Ladies in Trouble' or 'Certain Relief to Ladies' and suchlike. But only for a moment did you wonder, for while the law's penalties were severe, there was one major loop-hole. The only person — generally speaking, anyway — who could successfully bring a case against an abortionist would be the woman who had undergone the abortion. Who was just about the unlikeliest person in the whole world to do it. The shame of it, admitting you had wanted your own child killed in your womb! The horror of it, your name in the newspapers for the world to see! You'd never lift up your head in decent society again. So the abortionists flourished all over Manhattan, from Madame Restelle — Madame Killer, as she'd been known — with her fancy mansion on Fifth Avenue, down to the lowest vilest harpies on Chatham Square.

There were three classes of abortionist.

The ones who advertised themselves as 'Doctor', whether legitimate Doctors of Medicine or not — the newspapers which accepted their adverts never asked — the 'ladies' friend' with his 'infallible French pills' and his 'secluded rest-home' in the country for 'indispositions and female complaints'. They were received into the homes of the rich, and in many cases knew more of the skeletons in the family cupboard than the family's own doctor.

Mary wouldn't have been to one of those: they very rarely lost a patient. Besides, her clothes, while decent, had not been those of a wealthy or even comfortably placed woman.

The second and largest group were the female abortionists. Usually foreign, usually ex-nurses with some medical background or training. They were monsters, one and all, their only interest the money in a woman's purse. They called themselves 'Female Physicians' or 'Professors of Midwifery' and some of them were very, very rich.

Most of them had good houses uptown, with shabby little business premises downtown in the area west of City Hall Park.

The third class of abortionist were the butchers.

They were usually disbarred doctors, but often neither doctors nor nurses, just old men or women who didn't give a damn for sterilized equipment, drugs, painkillers or any of your fancy folderol. They were what Surgeon Gleason at the morgue had referred to as 'Second Avenue crochet-hook specialists.' His description fully explained their methods and their skills.

Frank O'Connor went up to Second Avenue.

He was east of the Bowery, deep in the heart of Monk Eastman's territory, but O'Connor wasn't too bothered by that. The Bowery gangs took no rake-offs from the abortion racket, and wouldn't take any notice of anyone inquiring into them. So Frank O'Connor checked every delivery firm, every removals yard, every wagoner's stable, every drayman and livery stable between Astor Place and Tompkins Square, south of Fourteenth and north of Houston, ticking them off one by one on the list he had copied from the voting register at City Hall. He worked carefully, methodically, unhurriedly east and then south and then west and then south and then east again. It took him two days until he found the man he was looking for.

His name was Stephen Askew.

He ran a small delivery firm at East 11th, just north of Tompkins Square, a wooden shed housing his two carts, with stalls off a little cobblestoned yard for the horses. When O'Connor came in off the street he saw a man raking wet, trampled straw out of one of the stalls towards the manure heap in the corner. There was a strong, familiar smell in the air and O'Connor suddenly realized it was the old farmyard smell he recalled from his boyhood, almost forgotten after all the years in the city.

'Howdy,' the man raking straw said.

'Mr Askew?' O'Connor asked.

'Inside,' the man said, jerking his head towards a hut on the side of the yard. It wasn't much more than a wooden shanty, with a dirt-grimed window. Inside Askew was bent laboriously over a grubby exercise book such as school-children use, writing with a stub of indelible pencil.

'Mr Askew?' asked O'Connor, tapping on the window.

'Aye,' Askew said, not looking up.

'O'Connor, Detective Corps.'

Askew looked up then, quickly, getting slowly off his stool and coming to the door of the hut.

'Police?' he said. 'What would ye want with me?'

'Just some routine questions, Mr Askew,' O'Connor said, reassuringly.

'Oh, aye? What about?'

'You keep a record of all your deliveries?'

'Aye, I do that.'

'Could you have a look at your schedule for September the eighteenth?'

'Sure, lad. What's it all about?' Askew sat down again on his wooden stool.

'Did you have anything for the Hudson depot over on West Thirtieth?'

'Indade I did, an' I don't need me book to tell me. Sure I took it over there meself, great hulkin' trunk that it was, an' it so warm.' He squinted shrewdly at O'Connor. 'Ye're goin' to tell me there was somethin' wrong with the trunk, now?'

'What makes you think that?'

'Well, I wondered about it when the woman gave me ten dollars to deliver it. Sure, I wouldn't charge more than three under normal circumstances, but — '

'What woman was this?'

'Up at this big house,' Askew said. 'On Sixth.'

'Number?'

'Six eighty-seven,' Askew said. 'Just opposite St Gabriel's Park.'

'All the way up there?' O'Connor was dismayed. His hunch had worked out right, but not for the right reasons. He hadn't known there were any abortion shops that far uptown on Second.

'Aye,' said Askew.

'Tell me what happened. In your own words.'

'Azey enough, lad. A woman comes into the yard, gives her name as Mrs Johnston. She's a trunk, she tells me, up at her house, to go across to the depot. She's a widow lady, she sez, takin' her few treasures back to Chicago by train. I'm to take the trunk to the depot, tell the baggage master to hold the receipt till she comes for it. 'Azey enough,' sez I.'

'And then?'

'She gives me the address, 687 Second, and I take meself up there the mornin' followin'. Ten dollars in cash, she gives me. 'T'ank you my man,' she sez. And off I goes.'

'You delivered the trunk to the depot?'

'Aye,' said Askew.

'Could you identify it again if you saw it?'

'Well,' Askew said, scratching his bald spot, 'that's a good one. Sure, there's plenty old trunks like that one kickin' about.'

'Would you be willing to come down to Headquarters and see it?'

'Aye,' Askew said. 'After I close up.'

'What time will that be?'

'Around eight.'

'You couldn't come before that?'

'Aye,' Askew said. 'If you've a mind to loan me a policeman to look after me yard and do me books while I'm gone.'

O'Connor grinned. 'Eight-thirty, say?'

'Aye,' Askew said. 'Now will ye tell me what all the fuss was about?'

'Sure,' said O'Connor. 'There was a dead body in the trunk.'

'Jesus!' Askew said, starting up from his stool so violently that he knocked it over backwards. 'Pathrick!' he yelled. 'PATHrick!' The man in the yard dropped his rake and came running as Askew clamped his billycock on his head and closed the exercise book on the desk.

'Yes, Mister Askew?' Patrick panted.

'Mind the place,' Askew told him. 'I've some business at Po-lice Headquarthers.'

Patrick looked as if he would have loved to ask why, but didn't dare.

'Well, then,' Askew said, looking at O'Connor, 'let's get at it.'

'Aye,' said the detective.

8

The newspapers were having a field day.

GHASTLY MURDER IN SPRING STREET, screeched the *Sun*. MANIAC KILLER CLAIMS SECOND VICTIM! shouted the *Herald*. SECOND MURDER — POLICE BAFFLED, stated the slightly less sensational *Times*. All of them carried highly coloured (and not particularly accurate) accounts of the finding of Katy Dawkins's body in the doorway behind the premises of Alton & Murdoch, Attorneys-at-Law of 744 Spring Street. Andy Nugent read them all dispassionately and then turned to the task of preparing a written report that was to be circulated to the captain of every precinct in the city, not to mention the mayor, his four commissioners of police, the superintendent, the chief of police, and every one of the twenty-eight detectives on the staff of the Detective Corps at 200 Mulberry Street. He worked methodically, referring often to the notes made by Surgeon Gleason and his own scribbled entries in the pocket notebook he used.

'MEMORANDUM [he wrote]
On Thursday, September 18, Patrolman James McCabe (Badge No. 486) discovered in an alleyway on West Third Street between Broadway and the premises of McBain and Hunter, a hardware store on W3rd, the body of a common prostitute Lilian Constance (Lily) Purcell. Post mortem examination revealed that the cause of death was the severing of the throat (see Surgeon Gleason's PMR No. 32) resulting in massive haemorrhage and death. The body of the woman was also massively mutilated by a knife or razor which Sgn Gleason (PMR 32) estimates would have been some four inches long. There was no evidence of abnormal sexual assault.

Subsequent investigations by the writer revealed that Purcell shared rooms at 139 Bleecker Street with another common prostitute named

Helen Wattis and had family in Baldwin City, Kansas, to whom the effects of Purcell were sent by the City upon request of the parents. A list of these (PDE 45) is attached.

Writer interviewed Sylvester George Henderson, 44, dry-goods wholesaler of 33 Sycamore Drive, Allentown, Pa, who had [he hesitated for a moment, searching for the right word] consorted with Purcell on the evening of the 18th and saw her on the night of the murder at approx. 11 pm. Purcell was talking to a man on the corner of Third and Broadway. Henderson saw them walk off down the street together. A description of the man as given by Henderson is attached (PIR 778).'

He stopped for a moment, reading over what he had just written. Yes, all the basic facts were there. He bent forward and continued writing.

'At just before eight am on the morning of Tuesday, September 25, Norman

George Logan, 19, clerk at Alton & Murdoch, Attorneys-at-Law of 744 Spring Street, opened the rear door of the premises and discovered the body of a woman. He summoned the police immediately. The first patrolman on the spot was again James McCabe (Badge No 486) on whose beat both murders have been committed. The woman was identified as Katherine Jane Dawkins, a common prostitute of no fixed abode. Inquiries are still proceeding to establish her domicile prior to death and family, if any. Post mortem examination revealed the cause of death to have again been severing of the throat (see Surgeon Gleason's PMR No 33) and the body had again been massively mutilated. As you will see from Sgn Gleason's report the wounds were more vicious and severe than in the case of Purcell, indicating, in Sgn Gleason's opinion, that perhaps the murderer stayed longer at his work than in the case of Purcell.

In the case of Dawkins, one major

piece of evidence was found at the scene of the crime. A note on plain white writing paper, approximately 4″ × 3″ was pinned to the woman's clothing with an ordinary safety pin. It was printed in block capitals with ordinary blue-black writing ink. It read as follows:

SO END ALL
OF THEM NIEMAND

The note is presently being photographed and copies of the photograph will be distributed to all recipients of this memorandum.

As in the case of Purcell, there was no evidence of abnormal sexual assault in the murder of Dawkins (see PMR 33).'

He stopped again, rereading; then he nodded and laid the sheet aside. Picking up another sheet, he started to write once more.

'Our most important evidence is the description of the man provided by Henderson and the note left on the

173

body of Dawkins. These should materially assist in the rapid apprehension and conviction of the murderer.'

He grinned to himself as he wrote this: political window-dressing, he thought, for the chief of police. Still, it had to be done: you always promised that an arrest was imminent.

'It is felt by Inspector Byrnes and other detectives with whom the undersigned has conferred that the murderer is a mentally unbalanced man whose killings are irrational and unpremeditated to the extent that while he seems to be selecting common prostitutes as his victims, there is no indication that he has any special woman or women in mind, but simply picks one up on the street and kills her. Secondly, it will not have escaped you that the name used to sign the note, 'Niemand', is German for 'Nobody'.

It is the undersigned's contention, therefore, that we are looking for a man of between forty and forty-five, well built, about five feet ten inches tall, wearing (possibly) a blue suit with a heavy gold watch-chain across the waist-coat. The man may be German or of German origin and special watch should therefore be kept in those areas where concentration of German immigrants is high.

It is also the undersigned's belief that the man may be living not far from the scene of both murders. It is possible, but not likely, that he could walk some distance on the side streets downtown with clothes which (see Sgn Gleason's PMR 33, note 2) would be extensively bloodstained. We may therefore safely postulate that either the man we are looking for wears a long coverall, or duster coat, or some kind of overall (which appears unlikely from the description given by Henderson) or he is able to disappear quickly from the scene of his crime into a nearby room or apartment and there remove the traces of his deeds. All personnel should therefore be advised to carry in their notebooks the PIR 778 given by

Henderson and maintain a vigilant search for this man.

Attached to this report, dated Wednesday September 26 are:

POST MORTEM REPORT 32 dated September 19

POLICE DECEDENT'S EFFECTS 45 dated September 21

POLICE IDENTIFICATION REPORT 778 dated September 21

POST MORTEM REPORT 33 dated September 25

All of which is respectfully submitted.'

Nugent leaned back and signed his name with a flourish. The paperwork was always the worst part, and for the moment, anyway, the worst part was over. He put the drafted report on the in-tray on Sergeant Bird's desk, and Bird grinned as he picked it up.

'I bet this ain't half as good reading as the story in the *Sun*,' he said.

'No,' Nugent told him. 'But it's a damned sight more truthful.'

'That's what I like about you, Andy,'

Bird told him. 'You're such a modest guy.'

'That's what I like about you, Sarge,' Nugent replied. 'How you can tell.'

★ ★ ★

Now they knew.

The man in the hotel room had all the newspapers spread out on the floor. He walked round the sad brown room drinking in the headlines, gloating again over the details. It had worked just as he knew it would. Niemand was in all the newspapers. Famous. Now every one of the marching legions of whores of Babylon, the shameless, abandoned ones who did it for money would tremble on their filthy sidewalks. The next man they smiled at might be Niemand.

He was proud of him, of his power.

Every shadowed alley they passed, Niemand might be hiding in. He would stalk the streets in their imagination, hiding in every doorway, every dark court, beneath every shaded tree. Niemand would lurk in every pool of blackness and they would be afraid. The headline on the front page of the *Times* especially pleased him. SECOND MURDER — POLICE BAFFLED! it said in forty-two-point caps. There was a dramatized woodcut block of the policeman McCabe finding the sprawled body, not very much like the real thing. There was a lot of detail, but very little fact. It was true, the police were baffled. Baffled! He savoured the word. But of course, they would be baffled. How could they find a phantom? Where could they search for Nemesis? How could they know when he would strike again? What could they do to stop him? Nothing! He chuckled. Niemand had them baffled, as you would expect. Niemand was the chosen instrument of the Lord's vengeance. No mortal power could intervene.

Let them try to find him.

He smiled. He wasn't angry today. The dark red spot somewhere in the back of his mind was not glowing, not pulsing. There was no need to worry about that today. Niemand would be there when he wanted him. He looked at the newspapers scattered on the floor. Reams and reams and reams of paper, all of it about Niemand. How many reams, how many founts of type, how many cans of printer's ink, how many reporters, how many editors, how many subs, typographers, artists, layout men, compositors, printers, delivery boys had been involved in bringing the story in this form before the eyes of the city? Thousands, he thought. He felt a glow of pride.

Then he took the gold watch from his waistcoat pocket and checked it. 7.40. No more time to look at yesterday's newspapers. Time for work. He picked the papers up, folding them carefully, and laid them on the table. Then he put on his jacket and went down the flight of stairs to the street. Niemand would wait for him in the room. He would understand. A man had to work, to eat. He had a good job and he didn't want to lose it. Niemand understood that. He respected skill, for he was a skilled worker himself. Nodding in confirmation of this, the man walked across to Broadway and took the streetcar uptown.

9

Quite a lot of it was Garibaldi's fault.

Joe Petrosino didn't blame him, of course. When Garibaldi had conquered Sicily and Naples in 1860 and turned his conquests over to the king of the Piedmontese the people of the Campania knew better than to wait around to see what would happen. Handing over the whole of southern Italy to those tyrants of the north was like tying up a tiger and delivering him to the goats, while at the same time providing the goats with steel teeth and claws. They had had enough of being torn apart by corruption and cynicism and exploitation already from their own people, which was bad enough. To allow Piedmontese to do it was unthinkable. So they left. They left in their millions, away from sunny Italy to the strange shores across the oceans: to Brazil, two million of them. To Argentina, where they founded the city of Buenos

Aires, another two million. And to America, bringing sunny Italy with them, for they knew no other way. They brought their *pasta*, they brought their *grappa*, they brought their Puccini, the jolly songs of the Neapolitan peasants, the life style of the *mezzogiorno*, the south. And when they arrived, they stayed Italian. It wasn't that they would not change: they couldn't. If you've grown up thinking all your life that anybody who isn't from your village is *straniero*, a foreigner, how can you adapt suddenly to a place where there are a million of them?

So they came off the boats at Ellis Island and ferried across to the Promised Land, where the educated Italians who had preceded them waited on the docks to recruit any *paesano*, fellow-countryman, who needed work into some kind of organized labour gang. Nobody complained. This was a welcome, of sorts, a straw of the old country to cling to in these drowning new sensations. This was the old *padrone* system, the boss system. That the *padrone* sold the *paesani* whom he had welcomed off the boat with cries of pleasure and embraces as part of a package to some American firm was politely not mentioned. Nor was the fact mentioned, if the *paesani* knew it, that the *padrone* took a cut off both ends of the joint: a commission from the firms to whom he supplied work gangs, and — of course — a contribution from the wages of his friends, his compatriots, for whom he had been able, after not inconsiderable difficulties in this new country, to find work immediately even when, as he politely pointed out, the *paesano* might not yet even know the language of his adopted land.

And the *padroni* begat the Little Italys. They helped to find their *paesani* places to live — for a commission at both ends. Where else would they go but where they were known, where they were expected, where they were *paesani*? To Mulberry Street, of course, and the streets all round it. To Little Italy. To where the Italians lived sometimes six to a room, eight to a room, ten to a room before they had enough money to rent a place for their own family, send money home so that their relatives could come over, put money down to buy a small business. A boot-black stand, maybe, or a little bakery. A cigar store, or a grocery. It was as if Italians had only one upheaval in them. Having crossed to the new land they could travel no more, no further. Here, unlike the Old Country, a man could work, feed his family, hope.

And it was in many ways just like home.

That was what Petrosino was finding out.

He had a job as a bartender in a place in Prince Street, and he'd grown a moustache. It wasn't that he expected any of the boys from Headquarters to come in: this was an almost totally Italian hang-out. Just somehow that he felt different, as if disguised, not his real self, with the heavy black moustache. He was a stocky man, about five feet eight, with a pockmarked face and snapping black eyes. He looked more Italian than half of the Italians in the place.

What he did was serve drinks. And listen.

All kinds of working men frequented the saloon. Dockwallopers, bricklayers, barbers, road-menders. After a few days he got to know some of their names. After a longer while he got to know other things. He got to know the names of the bordello-owners, the men you had to see on the docks if you wanted work, the loan-sharkers who would loan you five bucks on Monday provided you paid back six on Friday. He got to know the names of some of the men who had nice little rackets going down at the fish markets and the meat markets. It was damned slow work.

Every Friday night he would meet Inspector Byrnes in City Hall Park. He would tell Byrnes what he was doing. About the little box full of cards on which he wrote down the names, and anything he heard, whether ascertainable or not, about their professions, activities, employers. Byrnes was always interested, always made useful suggestions, but after their second meeting his mind was on other things.

They talked about the killings. They

were one of the most popular topics of conversation on Manhattan Island. Every man on the Force was looking for Niemand. There was a lot of pressure from the mayor, who was getting pressure from Albany, who were getting pressure from Washington.

It was three weeks since the murder of Katy Dawkins.

And no sign of the murderer.

Petrosino sympathized with the Chief, but when the expected hint that maybe catching Niemand was more important than finding out about some mythical secret society in Little Italy came, he ducked.

'I'm on to something big down here, Chief,' he argued. 'Let me follow through on it.'

'Dammit, Joe, I need every man,' Byrnes complained. 'We're overloaded in the worst way. Every nutty old lady in Manhattan is coming out the woodwork and telling us that her lodger is Niemand. Every maiden aunt some stranger bumps into in the street rushes into the nearest station house and tells the desk sergeant she's just been attacked by the Ripper.'

That was another name they were using. The Ripper. Maybe because it was a little less nebulous, a little more grim and real, than Niemand. The idea that the killer was Nobody was terrifying.

'You promised me time,' Petrosino told Byrnes.

'That I did,' sighed the Inspector. 'And I'll stand by my word. But Joe, if this maniac kills someone else, I may have to pull you off what you're doing.' He paused for a moment. 'I don't suppose . . . ?' he began.

'In Little Italy?' Petrosino grinned. 'You're kidding. They heard about the murders, of course. But they're not interested. They got jobs to do, kids to feed, letters from home with *real* news in them. They got their own problems. Believe me,' he added meaningfully.

Byrnes sighed again. 'Point taken,' he said.

They parted without any handshaking, not needing to say anything as fatuous as 'see you soon' or 'same time, same place next week?'. Their arrangement had been

186

simply made and was easily understood. Petrosino went to City Hall Park and fed the birds. If Byrnes could make it he would be there. If he couldn't then Petrosino fed the birds and went back to his room in Baxter Street, as he did now.

There was a piece of paper stuck on the door of his room with a thumb tack. It looked like this:

'Oh, sweet Jesus,' Petrosino said.

Although there was a city-wide hunt on for the murderer of the two prostitutes, it was not the only job the detectives had on their hands. Surveillance of the streets was best performed by the uniformed patrolmen, roundsmen and sergeants, who knew their precincts well and many of the residents in them. Their daily rounds on the beat often turned up surprising amounts of invaluable information about what was going on in the teeming streets of the city. Their reports were gone over each day at Mulberry Street and anything which might be of interest to the Detective Corps was passed over to Inspector Byrnes through channels. Meanwhile, the detectives themselves got on with the cases that had been so savagely interrupted by the two murders. As the days passed without incident the scare died down. People forgot. The newspapers had other sensations to report. Life went on.

A man was knocked down and robbed on West 23rd Street, his watch and money taken. He was very eloquent in his criticisms of a police force that left one of the better streets of the city to ruffians and footpads, and the newspapers gave him plenty of space to air his complaints. Byrnes put two of his detectives on the case, and within three days they had arrested the robber, a tenderloin tough named 'Dutch' Heinrich. The injured man was met outside the hospital by some friends of the arrested man, who described in graphic terms what would happen to him if he persisted in prosecuting. They offered him an alternative. He could have his watch and 50 per cent of the money back if he agreed to let the case drop. The gentleman thought it over very carefully for about three seconds and then went directly to Police Headquarters, where he advised them that he was dropping the case. Heinrich was released. He thumbed his nose derisively at the desk sergeant as he left the premises.

There were several complaints of robbery in dens of vice on Greene Street and round the Five Points. The tip of the iceberg, to be sure — most men robbed in the rooms of prostitutes hardly cared to draw attention to their sins by advertising them in a court-room — but sometimes the sum was enough to make them. The police called it panel thieving and knew it for a game as old as the profession that practised it.

The woman picked up her John and took him back to the shabby room in whatever house she worked for. She would recommend him to take off his jacket and trousers, and lay them over the back of a chair set against the wall. While she provided the fun and games he had come for, her pimp would slide back a panel in the wall and help himself to wallet, money, watch and anything else. More often than not, when it came right down to it, the victims would not prosecute in these cases, either. It was easier to tell your wife you'd had your pockets picked and leave it at that.

There was plenty of pocket-picking, too. On every streetcar line, in every crowded place, you'd find the dips, happily relieving fatter pigeons of their worldly goods. There was no quarter given in the world of the dips. Even a funeral was considered a useful place: the mourners were usually preoccupied, anyway, with thinking good thoughts about the dear deceased. Two of the dips, James 'Big-mouth Scottie' Day and Billy Jones, made the mistake of working one such funeral up at 120th and Fourth, only to find themselves confronted by a police captain who was attending it. One year each on Blackwell's Island at the Court of Special Sessions.

Let us not forget the drunks. From sunset until the small hours of Sunday morning every patrolman on the force is busy clearing drunks off his patch. Quiet drunks, noisy drunks, fighting drunks, argumentative drunks, sick drunks, drunks looking for another drink, a woman, a hand-out, a bed. All D & D's, drunk and disorderly, are arrested and thrown into the Bummers' Cells (and every station house has one of those). They shout a lot, they swear a lot, they fight a lot, they are sick a great deal, and they smell like a cesspit. There are around fifty thousand people arrested every year for D & D or A & B, assault and battery. There are also cases of assault with a deadly weapon (ADW) and intent to commit felonious entry (IFE) — burglary, if you prefer simpler terminology.

And then, of course, there is real crime.

So it wasn't as if the police and the Detective Corps had absolutely nothing much to do except keep an eye skinned for a man of about forty-five in a blue suit with a gold watch-chain, who might or might not be the Ripper, Mr Niemand, the Slasher of Spring Street or, as one whimsical reporter had called him, the 'Tart-cutter'. They had their work cut out on quiet days, when the worst that happened was a street accident caused by a runaway horse, or a parade of the Orangemen, or the rousting out of the river rats along the waterfront. They just kept at it.

As Frank O'Connor had kept on investigating the death of the woman who had been found in the trunk at the Hudson River Railroad depot. He was on his way uptown now with two patrolmen and three things going for him. The first was that the dead woman had been identified through an inquiry at the Department of Missing Persons. Her sister had come to New York from Paterson, New Jersey, where they had lived together. Her name was Muriel Worthington and her sister Audrey had left home some weeks before to come to the city. She had not written or sent word of her whereabouts and while at first Muriel Worthington had not been perturbed, after the second week she began to worry. Finally she came to the city and went to the Department of Missing Persons, and they, in due course, put the circumstances which she haltingly explained about her sister together with the description of the woman who had been found in the trunk.

So O'Connor knew that the dead woman had been Audrey Worthington of Paterson, New Jersey.

The second thing he knew was that the house at 687 Second Avenue was occupied by a Dr Jacob Rosenzweig, and that Doctor Rosenzweig had a thriving private practice. Dr Rosenzweig also employed a woman assistant who fitted the description of the Mrs Johnston who had hired the carter, Askew, to take the trunk from 687 Second Avenue to the railroad depot.

The third thing O'Connor had going for him was a search warrant.

So he knocked on the door of the imposing four-storey brownstone opposite St Gabriel's Park that sunny October morning with a fair degree of confidence that he might be getting near the end of this particular case.

The woman who opened the door was just as Askew had described her: middle-aged, dumpy, about five feet four, dark hair tied back in a neat bun, watery eyes that widened as she saw the two patrolmen standing on the steps.

'Yes?' she said, hesitantly.

'Dr Rosenzweig at home?'

'Er . . . no. He's away at present. I'm his housekeeper.'

'Your name, ma'am?'

'Waters. Elizabeth Waters. Mrs.'

'I'm Detective O'Connor,' the big man

said. 'This is Patrolman Jackson and Patrolman Clancy. And this — ', he took a folded piece of parchment from his inside jacket pocket, ' — is a search warrant.'

'S — search?' she said, drawing herself up a little. 'Search?'

'Would you like me to read it to you, ma'am?'

'No, of course not,' she snapped. 'I can read perfectly well.' She snatched the document from O'Connor's hand and glanced at it.

'What does this mean?' she asked.

'It means that I, and the issuing court, have reason to believe a felony may have been committed upon these premises and — '

'A felony?'

' — and am therefore empowered by the City and State of New York to enter and search the premises known as 687 Second Avenue — '

'What felony?'

' — there to conduct a search for such evidence as I believe may enable me to obtain a conviction or convictions of the person or persons responsible for said felony.'

'*What* felony?' she said, her eyes skittering from one man to the other, as if seeking the assistance any gentleman might offer a distressed gentlewoman. No such assistance was forthcoming.

'If you will stand aside, ma'am,' O'Connor said.

'No!' the woman said dramatically. She raised her arms and put her hands out palm forward as if to stop them by main force. O'Connor nodded to Clancy, and the patrolman neatly clicked a pair of handcuffs on to the thin wrists, slick as a whistle.

'Whaaat?'

O'Connor was already on his way into the vestibule. It was a light, bright hallway with a potted rubber-tree plant in a brass tub standing on one side, a half-table against the wall on which were scattered several visiting cards.

Patrolman Jackson led the woman inside, and sat her down on a chair that stood by the rubber-tree plant. She was mouthing shrill indignities, and Jackson patted her on the shoulder.

'Sure, you just sit there, ma'am, while we go about our business,' he told her. 'We'll do our best not to break anything.'

Then he closed, locked and bolted the door. If Mrs Waters tried to get out, handcuffed as she was, she'd make the devil of a noise with all those bolts and chains and things.

They started in the doctor's receiving room, and worked outwards from there. Clancy went to the top of the house and started in the attic. Jackson went down into the basement and began working his way up. They were there for nearly four hours. During that time they lifted, shifted, moved, checked, prodded, poked, tapped, knocked, sifted and sorted every single movable thing in the house.

The results of the search were simple, dramatic and conclusive. In the back of the house they found a sort of makeshift surgery: nothing fancy, but certainly adequate for the purposes for which they now knew Dr Rosenzweig used it. In the desk O'Connor found a cashbox with more than $2,000 in cash, and a number of receipt books and letter-heads in the name of Dr Aaron Ascher of 3 Amity Place. Dr Ascher-Rosenzweig was a methodical man. He kept a carbon copy of each receipt he issued. One of them was made out to Miss Audrey Worthington, Paterson, New Jersey, and was dated the day before the body had been found.

O'Connor sat in the leather-backed chair, not angry, not sad, not elated, not anything. Rosenzweig or Ascher or whatever his name was ran a respectable practice up here. Down at Amity Place he ran his butcher shop. He was patently guilty of the murder of the young woman from Paterson, New Jersey, but O'Connor had long since passed the point where murder angered him, and long since arrived at the point well beyond that where it saddened him. It was usually a tragic, pointless, futile, worthless, total waste of a good human life.

He got up and went out into the vestibule. Mrs Waters was still sitting in the upright chair near the door, her lips pressed together tightly. She looked ill.

'Where is Dr Rosenzweig, Mrs Waters?'

'He — he left town. On business,' she said.

'Mrs Waters,' O'Connor said gently, reprovingly.

'It's true,' she snapped.

O'Connor sighed.

'Mrs Waters,' he said, levelly. 'Dr Rosenzweig is a man who procures abortions, isn't he?'

The thin lips came together tight. She shook her head.

'He has an office downtown where he calls himself Dr Ascher?'

'I don't know anything about his business,' she said, her voice almost convincingly angry. 'I am the housekeeper here.'

'And you don't know a man named Stephen Askew?'

'Askew? No, I don't know anyone called Askew? Is he a patient?'

'He's a carter, Mrs Waters. He has a delivery firm down on East Eleventh Street.' He saw the reaction but said nothing as the woman got control of herself.

'I know no carters in that district or

anywhere else,' she snapped.

'And you've never used the name Mrs Johnston?'

Again the tight-lipped shake of the head.

'Mrs Waters,' O'Connor said, regretfully. 'I can send one of these men downtown now. He'll be back here in ten minutes with Askew. Do you want me to send for him?'

She stared at him for a moment. Then the tears came. He shook his head as Patrolman Clancy made as if to step forward, and stood impassively as the woman sobbed. She sobbed for perhaps three minutes, during which time neither O'Connor nor the patrolmen spoke. Finally she looked up, her eyes red, swollen, her nose running. She sniffed.

'Well, Mrs Waters?' O'Connor asked, gently.

'It's true,' she said.

'What's true, Mrs Waters?'

'I did it. I went down there. To that carter.'

'Why did you do that?'

'I told him I had a trunk to send as

baggage to Chicago, and could he come and collect it. I gave him ten dollars.'

'What was in the trunk?'

'You *know* what was in the trunk.'

'I want you to tell me.'

'A girl. A woman. She . . . she died. It was — oh, my God,' she sobbed. 'It was an accident, you've got to believe that. We try to take care, we — '

'Who is we, Mrs Waters?' O'Connor interrupted.

'The Doctor and — ' Her mouth fell open. She realized what she had just said. 'I — only brought him things. I never went in there. Never touched any of them.'

'There were many of them, Mrs Waters?'

'Three, four, sometimes more, every week.'

'Did any others die, Mrs Waters?'

She looked up at him and for a moment he saw right into her soul. And he knew real horror and disgust for the first time.

'You — they — what will happen to me?' she whispered.

'That's not for me to say, ma'am,' he said. 'That's up to the courts.'

'I only helped, I swear it!' she said. 'He'll tell you. You must find him and make him tell you!'

'Well,' O'Connor said, scratching his head like a bumpkin, 'I would if I knew where to start looking.'

'If — ' the woman said. She bit her lip, frowning.

'If?'

'If I — if I help you. Will that count in my favour?'

'Anything you do to assist the police will be duly noted, Mrs Waters,' he told her. 'But I can't promise you anything.'

'I see,' she said.

He let her sweat it out.

'He's with her,' she said finally. Her voice was flat, expressionless.

'Her?'

'That one. The floozy.'

'Can you tell me her name?'

'Miss High-and-Mighty Hoity-Toity,' the woman muttered. 'All airs and graces and the morals of an alleycat.'

'Her name, Mrs Waters.'

'Cunningham,' she said. 'Florrie Cunningham. An actress, she calls herself. She's only interested in him for his money. He can't see it, can't see that she doesn't care for him at . . . all.'

She faltered to a stop, tears in her eyes again. Good God, O'Connor thought, the poor woman's in love with the man! She knows he is a butcher and a murderer, and still she loves him.

'Have you any idea where they might be?' he said.

'They're at the Manhattan Beach Hotel,' she replied. 'Coney Island.'

And that was that.

★   ★   ★

'Impressive, isn't it?'

The young man nodded, without looking up.

'Surely is,' he drawled.

'Cost a million and a quarter,' the man said. He was an elegant-looking fellow, perhaps fifty-five or so, dressed in a pearl-grey suit with a matching Homburg hat and gloves. Grey buttoned spats fitted neatly over highly polished black shoes. He was carrying a copy of the *Times*.

'You're a stranger in town?' he asked.

'That's right,' drawled the young man. 'How'd you know?'

'I make it my business to judge a man by his appearances, sir,' said the elegant-looking fellow. 'You have to do that in my profession.'

'Oh, yeah,' said the younger man. 'What's that?'

'I own this steamship line,' the man said. 'Allow me to introduce myself: Stephen P. Jarvis, president of the Narragansett Steamship Company, the pride of whose fleet, the *Providence*, is the steamer at which you were looking.'

'Pleased to meetcha,' said the young man. 'Harvey Whitehill, of Kansas City, Kansas.'

'Here on business, Mr Whitehill?'

'Part business, part pleasure,' Whitehill said. He was a fair-haired, boyish-looking man, very slimly built and of medium height. He looked to be in his mid-twenties. He had been standing at the foot of the pier from which the NSC steamers left New York, gawping wide-eyed at the palatial boat for well over half an hour before Jarvis had approached him.

'It's a pity we didn't meet earlier,' Jarvis said. 'I could have shown you around the ship. Have you ever been on board a steamer?'

'Can't say I have,' Whitehill said.

'That's a shame,' Jarvis replied. 'Still, perhaps we could do it another day. The *Bristol* will be in tomorrow evening.'

'I'd like to do that, Mr, uh — '

'Jarvis, my boy, Jarvis.'

'Mr Jarvis. Thanks. If I can spare the time, I'd like to do that.'

'Busy schedule?'

'Pretty busy,' Whitehill said. 'Lot o' people to see.'

'I don't believe you mentioned what business you were in, sir?'

'Meat,' Whitehill said. 'I got me just about the biggest meat-packin' plant in Kansas City. Or the whole Midwest, come to that. Come to Noo York to fix up my contracts for next year. And maybe see a little night-life, know what I mean?'

'Precisely, my dear fellow,' Jarvis said. 'Precisely.'

'Well . . . ,' Whitehill began.

'Look here, Mr Whitehill — or may I call you Harvey?'

'Ev'body does,' Whitehill said.

'Harvey, then,' exclaimed Jarvis, enthusiastically. 'Have you any pressing engagement right at this moment?'

'Can't say I do,' Whitehill said.

'Well, my dear fellow, let us go up the street. There's a rather fine ah, waterhole, if I may say so, not more than two blocks away. It would give me great pleasure to stand you a couple of smiles.'

'Don't mind if I do, at that,' Whitehill said.

They walked up Albany Street towards Washington, Jarvis pointing out some of the larger business houses whose freight was carried on either the *Providence* or her sister steamer, the *Bristol*, and came to a large saloon which stood on the corner of Greenwich and Albany Streets. It was called The Steam Packet and many of its patrons wore the dark blue donkey jackets of stevedores and dock-wallopers.

It was pleasantly noisy, cool inside and smelling of sawdust. The bar was long and polished. Jarvis called the bartender across.

'A port wine for me, if you please,' he said. 'And for my friend here . . . ?'

'Beer will be fine,' Whitehill said.

'A schooner for my friend,' Jarvis said. 'Your good health, sir.'

'Mud in your eye,' said Whitehill.

He put his glass down on the bar with a smacking of lips, and as he did so a tall man in a dark business suit came across the room towards Jarvis.

'It's Mr Jarvis, isn't it?' he said.

Jarvis drew himself up to his full height, smoothing back the long grey hair at the side of his head.

'Yes, sir,' he said. 'What may I do for you?'

'You remember me, sir,' the newcomer said. 'Harrison, John Harrison? I worked in your offices, sir.'

'Ah, yes,' said Jarvis, obviously not remembering the man at all. 'Harrison. Well, what can I do for you, my dear fellow?'

Harrison looked embarrassedly at White-hill and said nothing.

'Come along, come along,' said Jarvis, a trifle impatiently. 'You can speak freely. This gentleman is a friend of mine.'

'Oh, well, sir,' Harrison said. 'Begging your pardon, like. Mr Jarvis, sir, I was wondering if you could help me out?'

Jarvis's patrician nostrils curled.

'Down on your luck, are you?' he said, as if it were the worst sin in the world. He started to fumble in his pocket, but Harrison stopped him with a nervous gesture.

'Oh, no, Mr Jarvis, sir,' he said, positively cringing, 'I wouldn't dream of askin' you for charity, sir.'

'Well, then?'

'Well, it's like this, Mr Jarvis, sir,' Harrison said. 'You were right to guess I've had a bit of bad luck. My wife took very poorly, you see, right after I lost my — right after I left your employ. There was doctors all the time, medicines to buy, and me out of work, like.'

'I'm sorry to hear that,' Jarvis said. 'Very sorry indeed. I hope the good lady is well on the road to recovery.'

'Well, that's just it, sir,' Harrison said. 'They tell me she's got to go convalescent to a place in Vermont. Tell you the truth, Mr Jarvis, I was at a loss to know what to do. Then I thought of you.'

'Now see here,' Jarvis said. 'I don't mind — '

'No, no, sir, nothing like that,' Harrison said. 'Here, let me show you.' He dug into his inside pocket and came out with a brown manilla envelope. From it he took an imposing-looking document with a heavy wax seal at the bottom. He handed it to Jarvis, who looked at it and then raised his eyebrows.

'Bless my soul,' he said. 'This is a certificate for a hundred shares in my steamship company!'

He looked at Whitehill, who returned his look with one of mild, but hardly concerned interest.

'How did you come by this?' Jarvis asked suspiciously.

'I saved hard when I was working for you, Mr Jarvis,' Harrison said anxiously. 'Every week I put money aside. When I had enough, I put it all into shares in the Company, sir. An investment, like, for when I retired.'

'How many of these have you got?'

'Just the hundred shares, sir,' Harrison said. 'And being down on my luck, like, and needing the money for poor Mary to go to the country, I wondered whether you might, well, if you would con-sider —?'

'Buying it back off you, you mean?' Jarvis said. 'But my dear chap, do you know what these shares are worth?'

'Well,' Harrison said.

'Let me tell you,' boomed Jarvis. 'The ordinary shares of the Narragansett Steamship Company are presently quoted on the Exchange at sixty dollars apiece. This certificate is worth six thousand dollars — less, of course, any broker's discount! I'm afraid — '

'Mr Jarvis, I'm in desperate straits,' Harrison said. 'Please, sir, make me an offer. Whatever you say the shares are worth, they're useless to me. I need cash money, and I need it quickly. You know as well as I do it would take a week to get the money on the Exchange.'

'You could take them to a bank,' Whitehill observed. 'Surely they'd accept the certificates as collateral against a loan?'

'That's a kindly thought, sir,' Harrison said, turning towards him. 'It's kind of you to interest yourself in my troubles. But you see, I'm an unemployed clerk. I live in lodgings. If I took this certificate to a bank, they'd think I'd stole it. That's why I've come to Mr Jarvis. He knows me, on account of I used to work for him.'

'Well,' harrumphed Jarvis. 'Now see here, Harrison, are you sure you know what you're doing? These shares are worth every penny of fifty-five hundred dollars even after a broker has taken his percentage.'

'Would you consider letting me have five hundred for them?' Harrison burst out. 'I mean, would — could you let me have five hundred in cash?'

'Well, see here, Harrison,' Jarvis said. 'I don't — ' He paused, and Whitehill saw a gleam of cupidity light up his eyes. 'Look, why don't you give me five minutes or so to think about it, what? Pop off around the block or something, and come back. I hate to even — '

'Oh, thank you, sir,' Harrison said. 'You're a real gent!' He turned and went out of the saloon, walking like a man who has just had the worries of the world lifted off his shoulders.

'Poor feller,' Whitehill observed. 'He must be in real trouble to sell that cheap. You goin' to buy?'

'To tell you the truth,' Jarvis said ponderously. 'I don't know. I mean, I'd like to help the fellow. Seem to recall now — we had to let him go through no fault of his own — you know how it is in business. But I — well, you're a businessman, Harvey, you'll understand. If I were seen to be trading in my own shares, buying up small lots on the Exchange, it might cause me a little embarrassment. Boardroom politics, what? My partners aren't too happy now about the fact that I hold a clear majority of the stock. If they were to see me apparently trying to get more, well — no need to go on, eh? Bartender, let us have the same again, here, if you please!'

The bartender bustled up and served another beer and a glass of port. Whitehill didn't speak until he was gone.

'You say them shares is worth over five thousand?' he said.

'Absolutely, my dear fellow. Here — ' He unfolded the *Times* and spread it out on the bar, smoothing out the page that listed the closing prices on the Exchange the day before. Running his finger down the tiny print, he stopped. 'There,' he said. 'Narragansett Steamship Company — good Lord, they're up three points! Six hundred and four cents a share! And rising, by the look of it!'

Whitehill shook his head.

'Seems like a hell of an opportunity to let slip through your fingers. You know, I — ' He stopped and shook his head.

'Naw,' he said.

'Why, my dear fellow, are you interested?' Jarvis said. 'I mean, I had no idea that you might have the slightest interest in stocks and shares.'

'Oh, I kind of keep an eye on a few

things,' Whitehill said. 'The beef business ain't what you'd call reliable. Sometimes pays a man to lay off a bet here and there.'

'By George, you're right,' said Jarvis, clapping him on the shoulder. 'Man after my own heart. Real businessman, I can always tell.'

'Well, then?'

'You really want to buy the shares?'

'Let me put it to you this way: I'd admire to make a clear profit of five thousand dollars on a ten-minute deal.'

'Who wouldn't?' Jarvis agreed, jovially. 'But see here, I think you ought to cut me in on it.'

'Why?'

'Well, after all, Harvey, you'd have never even known about this fellow Harrison if it hadn't been for me.'

'True,' admitted Whitehill. 'But you can't buy the shares anyway. You just said so.'

'That's right,' Jarvis agreed ruefully. 'You've got me over a barrel. Even so, with you as nominee, I could get in on the deal. I mean, fair is fair, old chap.'

'Not in business,' Whitehill said. Before Jarvis could reply they saw Harrison come in through the door of the saloon. He gave himself a moment to get accustomed to the gloom and then his face lit up as he saw both men still standing by the bar.

'Mr Jarvis,' he said, hurrying across. 'I was afraid you might have left, not had the heart to turn me down.'

'My dear fellow,' Jarvis said.

'Well, Mr Jarvis? Will you buy?' Harrison pulled the envelope from his pocket and held it out.

'Now see here, Harrison,' Jarvis said. 'The thing is — '

Harrison's face fell. 'You don't want to buy?'

'Well, not exactly,' Jarvis said. 'You see, my dear fellow, I haven't five hundred on me, and since it's well after three, the banks are already closed.'

'Oh,' said Harrison. He stood there with his shoulders slumped, the very picture of total dejection.

'You wouldn't sell them to me, would you?' Whitehill said.

Harrison looked up, puzzled. His eyes shuttled from Whitehill to Jarvis, and back, and back again.

'I — I don't understand. Mr Jarvis,' he said.

'Ah, Harrison, this gentleman is Mr Harvey Whitehill, of Kansas City, Kansas. When we were discussing your shares, he expressed an interest in buying them.'

'You . . . you want to buy them, too?'

'Well,' Whitehill said. 'You can sell 'em to Mr Jarvis here. But you wait until tomorrow. Alternatively,' he added, reaching into his inside pocket and bringing out his wallet, 'you can sell 'em to me now.' He opened the wallet wide and the two men saw it was full of currency.

'Wee-e-e-ll,' Harrison said hesitantly.

'Oh, go ahead, my boy,' Jarvis boomed suddenly. 'It's not as if I need the money. Lose more than that in a week at Morrisey's anyway,' he chuckled, nudging Whitehill.

'Five hundred, you said?' the Kansan asked.

'If — if Mr Jarvis says it's all right,' Harrison said.

'Of course, of course,' Jarvis boomed.

Whitehill counted ten $50 bills out on to the counter and Harrison picked them up. He handed Whitehill the manilla envelope. 'Here's your certificate,' he said. 'And thank you, mister. Now I can see that my wife is properly taken care of.'

'In about three years you can,' Whitehill said.

Harrison's head jerked up at the change in Whitehill's voice. Gone was the drawling accent, gone the loose-limbed stance. Before him was a narrow-eyed young man with a Police Positive revolver in his hand.

'Wh — what is this?' Harrison said.

'It's called a pinch, a fair cop or a collar,' Whitehill said. 'It comes out the same whatever you call it.' He reached into his pocket and pulled out the copper detective's shield which he pinned on his lapel.

'Detective Edward Slevin,' he said. 'You're both under arrest.'

'See here, my man,' Jarvis said. 'You are making a terrible mistake. I am — '

'You are Michael Bateman, alias

Colonel Robert E. Lee Devereaux, alias Stephen P. Jarvis,' snapped Slevin. 'You want me to recite the rest of your record?'

The distinguished-looking Bateman sighed.

'What a shame, David,' he said to his accomplice. 'Just when we were doing so well.'

'It's all downhill from here,' Slevin told him.

10

It was as sweet a job as ever was pulled.

One-Lung Curran took to the idea like a duck to the water, and the Dusters knew that their campaign of vengeance was in good hands once One-Lung got interested.

He was a beanpole of a boy, One-Lung was, tall and stringy and as pasty as a floured pancake due to the tubercular condition that had reduced his breathing capacity by half and given him his Hell's Kitchen sobriquet. He worked, on and off, as a messenger boy for the railroads, but more off than on. In between, due to his meagre width, he was much in demand as an assistant on burglaries, on raids upon freight cars in the Hudson River yards and, during the winter, as a marvellous means of getting the rich mugs on the Avenue and Broadway to part with their small change. One look at One-Lung shivering in the December wind on the corner of 42nd Street, his big watery blue eyes accusingly pathetic, and it was the hardest-hearted widow-squeezer in New York who could pass him by without throwing something into his tattered cap. On a really bleak day, One-Lung could pick up as much as $3 or $4 this way, and that was an achievement to be saluted by any man.

He had one other thing going for him (vital in affairs of the kind the Dusters were planning). He wasn't known to the saloon-keepers down on Greenwich Street, which was where the ball was to open.

The Dusters, now, knew as much about the procedure of the Police Department as the police themselves. They had to, for sometimes their livelihood and freedom depended upon knowing which patrolman was on duty, what his beat was and his likely reaction to seeing whatever they might be up to. Sure, there were one or two you could square with a fresh ham stolen from the 30th Street yards, or a case of Irish that had 'inadvertently fallen into the docks' on the lower North River.

But it was a byword everywhere on the West Side that you never, never, never trusted a copper.

The hours of duty for patrolmen were divided in a rather strange manner: from 6 to 8 am; from 8 am to 1 pm; from 1 o'clock until 6 o'clock in the evening; from 6 o'clock until midnight; and the graveyard shift, midnight to 6 o'clock the following morning. These 'tours' were planned out on a duty board which, so far as had ever been ascertained, nobody, including the Commissioner himself, had ever been able to understand. But the basic idea was that no patrolman would ever be called on duty at the same hour on two successive days. However, it wasn't difficult to work out with a fair degree of accuracy which patrolman would be on what tour if you knew two things: one, was he on day or night shift, and two, what was his first tour of the shift?

It took the Dusters about two hours to find out that Patrolman Dennis Sullivan was on the day shift, and that his tour on the first day was 6–8 in the morning, and

1–6 in the afternoon. Which meant that next day he had to be on the 8–1 and 6–midnight tours, right?

Right.

It was all set for the 6–midnight. They wanted everyone to see this. They knew Sullivan's beat route off by heart. Out of the station house and turn right, down Charles to Washington, south a block and right again, checking out the boat stores along the waterfront, left at Christopher and up as far as Bedford Street, turning right down Bedford and back to Hudson Street along Grove. Down Hudson as far as Houston, then left up to Seventh Avenue, up Seventh to Morton, left on Morton and across to Washington again, then down Washington to Clarkson, over on Clarkson to Greenwich and back up Greenwich six or seven blocks to the station house. They knew what he would be looking for: it was all in the *Police Manual*. Anybody trying to pull a dip — pick a pocket. Anybody maltreating an animal — horse, cow, dog or cat — in a public place. Anybody carrying a firearm, a visible club, a slingshot or other deadly or dangerous weapon. Any dogfights, prizefights or cockfights staged for the purpose of wagering. Anybody destroying or defacing private or public property. Anybody (openly) gambling. And, of course, the usual felonies and misdemeanours: D & D, A & B, ADW and IFE. In addition, he was to examine doors, windows and gates of houses and business premises on his beat, and to advise the owners or occupants of such premises if any were open or unlocked; to keep an eye out for policy dealers, gamblers, fences, receivers, thieves, vagrants and other known offencers, as well as to watch all known disorderly houses, brothels, houses of assignation or flops and note the persons frequenting them.

In other words, the patrolman was kept fairly busy on his beat just keeping up with the requirements of his job, if he was a genuine (read 'honest') cop. There were plenty, of course, who turned blind eyes towards much of the aforementioned. They were the ones who could be bought off for a weekly 'contribution' from unlicensed saloon-keepers or the even fouler cellar shops, for a quick jump with one of the girls, for a pay-off on the proceeds of the crap games or the policy numbers or, generally speaking, a piece of the action.

Patrolman Dennis Sullivan, Badge No. 377, was not one of these.

Consequently, when it was known that he was on his rounds, the whores quietly faded off the street until he'd passed, the policy dealers called in their local saloon for a smile, the cellar shops closed their doors, and the dips kept their hands in their own pockets. After all, who needed aggravation?

One-Lung Curran, that's who.

He went into Mick Dwyer's saloon at the corner of Morton and Greenwich at about nine o'clock and ordered a beer. The place was pretty full for a Tuesday night, with the usual arguments going on about horses, prizefighters, wages and the cost of living — it had been said in the paper only the other week that those who aspired to live in comfort and in a respectable neighbourhood in New York could not do so on less than $5,000–$6,000 a year, a figure which, to the *habitués* of Mick Dwyer's saloon, was about as attainable as the moon, and never mind the figure of 15–20 grand that had been quoted for the family that wished to live fashionably. These were men who were earning less in a month than it cost to rent two rooms and a parlour in the Fifth Avenue Hotel for a day.

Curran, however, was not really concerned with the cost of living, the relative merits of racehorses, prizefighters or easy lays. He stood by the bar, staring into the ornate mirror behind the bar, watching the swing doors opening to Greenwich Street. It was one of those mirrors that the breweries used to supply with ornate gold lettering advertising its wares. 'SPUYTEN DUYVIL BEERS,' it modestly proclaimed, THE BEST IN THE WORLD — BREWED IN NEW YORK CITY.' It was about six feet wide, and almost as high. It was surrounded by an ornately carved wooden frame with little wooden angels at the top two corners.

One-Lung saw in it what he'd been looking for. In the doorway the familiar face of Marty Brennan peeping over the top of the doors and grimacing furiously. One-Lung nodded, and emptied his beer tankard on to the bar. Then he tapped the shoulder of the big Irish labourer standing next to him. The man was six feet two if he was an inch, and he turned at One-Lung's persistent pecking at his shoulder, a frown on his face.

'You knocked my drink over,' One-Lung told him, gesturing with his chin at the spreading pool of beer on the bar.

'Oi did what?' growled the navvy.

'You knocked over my beer,' One-Lung said to him. 'So you'd better pay up for another.' He was awfully polite about it, but there was a note of righteous determination in his voice, too.

'Oi niver did onny such ting,' the astonished Irishman said. 'D'yez hear what he's sayin'?' he asked his assembled friends.

'You did so,' One-Lung said. 'You big Mick.'

Now if you happen to be Irish, you'll

know there are certain things that Irishmen joke about among themselves, these being principally drinking, sex and religion. They laugh uproariously at almost anything one of their own kind says to them (unless, of course, he's a Protestant and they're Catholic, in which case all bets are off) and are, by and large, a tolerantly inclined race. However, there are certain rules for handling relationships with Irishmen. You never, for instance, cast the remotest aspersions upon the virginity of the most raddled Irish whore in Manhattan. You do not, under any circumstances, make slighting remarks about the Irish tendency to overestimate the amount of alcohol they can consume in any given period of time. You never, never make jokes about the sex lives of priests and nuns (although they may do so among themselves with complete impunity). And most of all, you never call one a big Mick, unless you are thoroughly prepared for what will inevitably happen next.

One-Lung Curran was ready, and so when the Irishman's huge fist came thundering round in a haymaker that would have taken off One-Lung's head had it landed, the slim youngster ducked neatly beneath it and whipped a nasty kick right into the Irishman's shin. The Irishman let out a whoop of pain and — as One-Lung had foreseen — abandoned his intention of separating One-Lung from his immortal soul for the more immediate pleasure of jumping up and down on one foot and loosing off a string of oaths that would have melted the ears of any genteel lady in ten seconds flat. At this moment One-Lung hefted the heavy glass beer tankard carefully and, taking deliberate aim, threw it with all his strength straight at the big mirror on the wall.

Even as the mirror shattered with the most appalling crash of glass — and outraged shouts from the astonished bartender — One-Lung was darting towards the door and out into the street, where he ran straight into the arms of Patrolman Dennis Sullivan, who was running towards the sound of the altercation, which was clearly audible in

Greenwich Street.

'Hold on there, now!' shouted Sullivan, twisting One-Lung round by the arm.

'By all means,' said One-Lung, politely, and twined his arms round the patrol-man's body. His long, sinewy legs came off the ground and up behind Sullivan's knees, and the two of them went down on the cobblestones with a thump that could be heard clearly by the men spilling out of Mick Dwyer's saloon, fists cocked and ready for action.

'Stand back, the lot of yez!' yelled Stumpy Mallarkey, who was now in the centre of the street. He had a short piece of four-by-two timber in his hand, up and ready to use as a club. 'This is Dusters' business!'

The word 'Dusters' stopped the boiling crowd of men in their tracks, and they reared back as out of every doorway in the street a crowd of red-shirted, white-neckerchiefed ruffians raced across to where Patrolman Dennis Sullivan was vainly trying to disentangle himself from the cat-like clutches of One-Lung Curran.

Then with one quick jump One-Lung let go of the policeman and got clear. Sullivan was on one knee when he saw the Dusters coming at him, and he fumbled desperately for his whistle, but he was a good sixty seconds too late.

Newburgh Gallagher got in the first blow, and it was a terrible one. With Sullivan on one knee, Newburgh set himself well and hit the patrolman squarely in the face with his fist. In the clenched fist Newburgh was holding a short round piece of iron, about an inch in diameter. It turned his fist into a lethal weapon and the shouting spectators on the sidewalk saw Sullivan's face dissolve into a mask of bright red blood. He went up slightly and then back and down, and the Dusters — eight, nine, ten of them — swarmed all over him. The watchers heard Sullivan give a terrible roar of rage, saw him toss two of the Dusters off his back as though they were flies, struggling to his knees, almost making it upright, but sheer weight of numbers was against him. The Dusters hit him again and again and again and again. All of them had something hard or something heavy in their hands, and one or two of them had good solid, heavy steel-capped mining boots as well. The sounds of the blows hitting Sullivan's body were flat, meaty, awful things to hear, the sound you hear when a butcher takes an axe to a side of beef. It was over in about twelve minutes. Then the Dusters got up off the bleeding hulk of Patrolman Dennis Sullivan, spreading away from it like carrion birds leaving the bones of some fallen animal. One or two of them had marks on their faces. Stumpy Mallarkey had a bleeding nose. They stood all in a bunch in the middle of the street, the people on the sidewalks who had watched the carnage suddenly awed into silence by the sight of what they had done to Sullivan.

His face was pulped, unrecognizable. His uniform jacket was almost completely ripped off, and one of his legs lay at that peculiar angle which could only mean it was broken. From the mess that had once been his mouth, Sullivan emitted a mewling, gutted sound of agony as he writhed on the filthy cobblestones. 'Jesus

God Almighty,' someone whispered. But nobody moved. The Dusters in strength and in a fighting mood were too much of a war for anybody in this part of the world to fight voluntarily, and especially for a policeman.

'All right!' yelled Happy Jack Mullraney. 'Somebody find a cart!'

He stood there in the centre of Greenwich Street, that death's-head smile daring anyone to challenge him or his cohorts. No one moved. They watched as one of the Dusters trundled a handcart across to where Sullivan lay, watched as the groaning man was lifted and tossed unceremoniously into the cart, and stood watching as the Dusters, chanting and singing now, gathered round the cart, which they pushed up Greenwich Street towards the station house.

Inside two blocks it turned into a procession. Every kid in the soot-streaked tenements turned out to follow the Dusters, every street sparrow in the neighbourhood ran to join the throng, and soon, by the time they were six blocks uptown and near the station house itself, there were anything up to two hundred chanting, jeering, shouting, lurching, yelling, pushing, hooting West Siders of every age, shape, size and denomination following the cart in which the now unconscious Sullivan lay. Somewhere along the way one of the Dusters had appropriated a flat sheet of cardboard and on it had daubed the words 'A TUF COP' — a derisory challenge to all the other tough cops who might think they could treat the Hudson Dusters in the cavalier manner in which Patrolman Dennis Sullivan, Badge No. 377, had imagined he could.

By the time they reached the corner of Charles Street the word had spread ahead of them, and a cordon of patrolmen was coming out of the station house on the trot.

'All right, lads!' Happy Jack shouted, still smiling. 'Beat it!'

The Dusters — and everyone else who had followed them — were absolutely expert at getting off the streets fast and out of the way of the cops. The crowd melted before the advancing blue line as if it had been butter beneath a desert sun, leaving the handcart with its twin handles tipped towards the sky and the now stripped, naked, bloody, broken body of Dennis Sullivan sprawled groaning in the middle of the intersection. Gone were his coat, his pants, his belt, his club, his badge, his pistol. Gone his underwear, his wallet, his whistle, his notebook, gone somewhere in the melting cohorts fleeing now as the policemen started running towards the figure of their fallen comrade. The only other thing left in the empty street was a piece of torn cardboard which lifted in the wind and skated towards the gutter. 'A TUF COP,' it said, on one side. On the other, neatly hand painted by the shopkeeper from whose store-front it had been stolen, it said: 'EVERYTHING MUST GO.'

★   ★   ★

They came in the night and if he had been in the bed they would have taken him. Both men were big, heavy, moving fast as cats on their feet as they silently opened the door. The first one hit the fine wire that Petrosino had stretched across the room and fell grunting, retching, and Petrosino moved fast as the other stopped, confused, smashing him down with a viciously placed blow from the leather-covered blackjack. The man went down on the floor like a sack, soundless, blood seeping from his right ear. Petrosino stepped across his still form and hit the other man in the face as hard as he possibly could.

He felt bone go, and the man went backwards against the thin wooden wall, shaking the building, his swarthy face suddenly bright with blood. Petrosino stood over him, swaying, breathing heavily. His knuckles were bleeding.

The man looked up at him with bright, beady, malevolent eyes and started to get to his feet. Petrosino hit him again. He felt no compunction. It was like hitting an ox.

The man went back down again on the grimy floor. He was almost unconscious. He smelled. Petrosino lugged him on to the bed and lashed him to the bedposts

X-wise, ankles and wrists. The man on the floor groaned and Petrosino went quickly across the room. He lashed the other man's hands and feet with what they called a 'Chink's knot', a means of tying a man by which, should he attempt to wrestle with his bonds, he would rapidly choke himself to death. It worked much on the principle of the choke-chain people use for dogs.

Then he picked up the jug of water on the washstand and threw it in the bleeding face of the man on the bed. Spluttering, cursing, the man surged upwards against the rope. He realized quickly what had happened and subsided on the soaking bedclothes, only the dark eyes alive and full of hate.

'Who are you?' Petrosino said in Italian.

The man tried to spit at him through his broken lips.

'*Da dove viene lei*?' Petrosino said. 'Where are you from?'

Again the man raised his head and tried to spit. Petrosino hit him, not too hard, with the back of his hand, a stinging, driving blow that racked the man's head sideways, a dull suffused welt slowly appearing on his right cheekbone.

'Who sent you?'

Nothing.

'Who sent you?'

Nothing.

Petrosino hit him hard in the belly and the man's body contorted against the bindings, a drool of green spittle trickling out of his swollen mouth. He shook his head.

'Okay,' Petrosino said.

For the first time a faint frown of worry appeared on the face of the man on the bed. Petrosino's voice was so reasonable, so ordinary, that it was more frightening than any violence. He lay unmoving as Petrosino went through his pockets, tossing wallet, key-chain, folding knife, medallions, small change, handkerchiefs on to the washstand. Then he followed the same procedure with the unconscious one on the floor. This one had a pistol, an old Starr .38. Petrosino pursed his lips thoughtfully. He picked up the pistol and hefted it in his hand. It was a solid, heavy weapon, fully loaded. He looked at the man on the bed. The man looked back at him, trying to be impassive, but there was an edge of anxiety in the way he was holding his body.

'You won't tell me who you are?' Petrosino asked.

The man shook his head: no.

'Or who sent you?'

No again.

'Okay,' the detective said in that reasonable tone. He went over to the bureau and got an old wool shirt out of the drawer. Wadding it into a thick ball, he laid it against the knee of the man on the floor. He looked up to make sure the man on the bed could see what he was doing. The man was watching with horrified eyes. He knew. Petrosino nodded. Good.

He laid the wadded shirt against the man's leg and pressed the barrel of the gun against it and into the wad. Then he pulled the trigger. The man was deeply unconscious, but he screamed aloud, a shrill, raking shriek of physical agony, his body twisting against the ropes that bound him. Petrosino held the bonds to make sure the man wouldn't choke himself. His face was as if carved from stone. Then he got up and walked over to the bed. He laid the smouldering shirt against the leg of the man on the bed. The man involuntarily tried to move his leg away but the bonds were firm.

'Would you like something to bite on?' Petrosino asked politely.

'No,' said the man. 'No, no, no!'

'Okay,' said Petrosino. His voice was still reasonable, friendly.

He cocked the pistol and the man screamed.

'Talk!' said the detective.

He could hear a commotion now on the landing outside his room, and in another moment someone hammered on the door.

'What's happening in there?' someone shouted. It sounded like old Sollozzo, the landlord.

'Get the police!' shouted Petrosino. 'There's been an accident.'

'What's happening?' shouted someone else.

'Get the police!' he heard Sollozzo tell them. He could imagine the old man standing there in his undershirt, braces hanging round his hips, the whitened moustache stained with tobacco juice, jaws chomping on his perpetual cud. 'Get the police! *Avanti, avanti!*' Feet thundered down the stairs. Petrosino could still hear the sound of voices outside on the landing. They weren't going to miss a free show like this. They would wait until the patrolman arrived to see what was going on. There'd been a shot, someone said. Who had been shot? Why? Was it someone they knew? Someone in the house? Who? They would wait. And they folded their arms and waited.

Petrosino turned back to the man on the bed.

'Talk,' he said again.

The man on the bed grinned.

'You're stuck, copper,' he said. 'You're stuck. In ten minutes a big fat Irish cop will come bustin' in through that door and askin' questions about who shot who and why.'

'How did you know I was a copper?'

'We got our ways.'

'We?'

'We.' The eyes narrowed, hooded with venom. 'You saw the sign.'

'You mean the Black Hand? I thought the *Camorra* was dead.'

'Well, you know what thought did. He only thought he did.'

'What?'

'It's an old Neapolitan saying, copper.'

'You're stalling.'

'That's right,' the man said, grinning again.

'Who sent you?'

'Father Christmas,' the man said.

Petrosino cocked the pistol again, and the man flinched at the triple click. He managed to hold the sneer on his face.

'Listen, copper,' he said. 'You got the Black Hand message. That means you're dead unless you listen to reason.'

'What reason?'

'Sense,' the man said urgently. 'Listen to sense. No point in stirring everything up, poking your nose where it don't need to go. Listen, we wasn't going to kill you.'

'Just break my bones a little, you mean?'

'Nah, nothin' like that. We was comin' to take you to The Man. He wants to talk to you.'

'What man?'

'The Man, for Godsakes,' the man on the bed said. 'The Don.'

'The Don?'

'Christ, you act dumb for someone supposed to be a detective.'

'Okay, I act dumb. What Don?'

'Don Gabriele. He's the man of respect down here. Didn't you know that?'

'No.'

'Jeez, it's just like the Don says,' the man told him. ''The cops are so stupid,' he says. 'They do not know I exist. And even if they did, there is no law broken, no reason for them to even ask me a question.''

'Where does he hang out, this Don Gabriele?'

'Not far from here. Look, cut me loose, and I'll take you to him. We can pay the cop off. He knows me.' Petrosino made a mental note of that.

'Suppose I don't want to talk to Don Gabriele?'

'Jesus, even you ain't that stupid, are you?'

'Supposing I am?'

'Then you're a dead man,' was the flat reply. 'You'll wake up one morning with half of your fucking head missing.'

'My, my,' Petrosino said. 'Is that what you tell the old cobblers and grocers you and your pals terrorize?'

'Nah, we — ' The man looked up suddenly. 'Hey,' he said.

'You're the muscle, right?'

No reply.

'You're the boys who follow up on orders, see to it people stay in line, set off an explosion here, smash up an old man's hand there. That it?'

Again no reply.

'Boy,' Petrosino said wonderingly. 'You're some *paesano*, I'll tell you.'

'Ah, go to hell,' the man said. 'We was told to reason with you. If that failed, we was told to mess you up. Okay, you stopped us this time. But next time . . . '

He let the threat hang in the air.

'What's your name?' Petrosino asked, apparently unperturbed.

'Why?'

'I might need it for your grave stone,' Petrosino said.

'Funny,' sneered the man.

'Not as funny as the idea of you coming after me again,' Petrosino told him.

'How do your work that out, copper?'

'On crutches?' Petrosino said, and shot him in the leg. The man's agonized scream was still echoing round the room when the patrolman burst the door down and came into the room like a bull coming into a bull-ring. He hauled up short at the sight in front of him. By the door a man was lying in a pool of his own blood. Another man on the bed was writhing and twisting and screaming, the right leg of his trousers soaked in blood which was staining the tangled bedclothes beneath him. And by the window stood Joe Petrosino, the revolver in his hand still smoking.

'All right, you,' growled the patrolman, his hand on the butt of his own revolver.

'Hand that gun over, nice and careful, now!'

Petrosino grinned and handed over the pistol butt first. Outside in Baxter Street he could hear the bell of the paddy wagon as the horses clattered to a halt. In ten minutes he was inside Police Headquarters, and in another ten in Byrnes's office.

'Joe,' Byrnes said. 'What the hell happened?'

'I hate to tell you this,' Petrosino said with a grin, 'but I lost my job.'

★　★　★

Patrolman James McCabe, Badge No. 486, was fed up.

It was more than three weeks since he had found the bodies of the two prostitutes and the boys at the station house were still kidding him about it. He'd come in off duty and the desk sergeant would heavily say something about his report: 'What, no stiffs today, Jimmy?' He'd go tiredly upstairs to the dormitory on the first floor and whoever was there would call out something along the same lines.

'Find any dead ones, Jim?'

'Nobody cutting up on your patch, son?'

'Very funny,' he'd say, trying to stifle his annoyance. 'Very funny.'

They hadn't seen the Grand Guignol he had. They didn't wake up some nights in a cold sweat seeing the blood, the staring wounds. His wife Patsy said it was beginning to prey on his mind. Maybe it was, he thought. It would on anybody's.

Not only that, he'd had a dressing down from the Captain himself. As if it was his fault the whores had let themselves be killed on his beat. 'The occurrence of crime on the streets,' the Captain (quoting the *Manual*) had said sententiously, 'is always regarded as presumptive evidence of negligence on the part of the patrolman in whose beat such crime is committed.'

Well, the hell with them all.

And to hell especially with Harry Seeley, the precinct roundsman, who'd jokingly suggested that maybe Jimmy was the Slasher himself — after all, he'd the same general appearance as the official description that had been printed up and circulated throughout Manhattan. Well, it was true as far as it went. James McCabe was forty-three, and he was solidly, sturdily built. He did wear a blue suit, of a kind, and it did have a chain across its front (but not gold, just steel, with a whistle on the end of it, not a gold watch). And he was more or less the same height as Mr Nobody — five nine in his stocking-feet.

However, he wasn't the Slasher. He was a good, reliable Irish cop who'd served the Force well for nearly fifteen years, and he'd seen plenty in his time. He'd been in the Force during the 1873 panic, and he'd helped to clear the streets of dead and wounded after the Irish riots some years before that. He'd made his share of arrests — his beat, which stretched for three blocks on both sides of Broadway from Union Square down to Houston Street had its share of the rougher side of Manhattan low life. All of which conspired to make him feel thoroughly fed up with the whole job and wish he'd chosen some other line of business like his brother Terence, who was well on his way to being a successful building contractor in Brooklyn, with a nice big house on State Street with a back yard that had a little patch of lawn and flower borders. And as if that wasn't enough, he'd pulled the night shift on the week's duty roster, and if there was anything guaranteed to make a man absolutely, thoroughly fed up, it was having to police the empty streets south of Union Square in the small hours of the morning. Especially a Monday — well, Tuesday morning, actually. It was — after Sunday — one of the quietest days of the week. From Thursday on, things hotted up on Broadway, but Mondays many of the restaurants and clubs were closed, cleaning up after the hectic weekend, getting back into some kind of shape for the week ahead. The crowds were thinner, the number of carriages and cabs and wagons fewer. Over here on Wooster there were few enough people about at all, and his main concern was checking the gates and doors of the small shops and offices and lodging houses as he went along.

At first he thought the woman was drunk.

She reeled towards him as he turned left round the corner into Houston Street, one hand in front of her like a blind person who's lost his stick, weaving in a curious, shambling walk along the wide sidewalk. He lifted his lantern high and moved towards her, and as he did she screamed, a thin, high, terrified scream, and slumped to the ground, crouching huddled away in what looked like panic.

'Now, now, Missis,' he said. 'No need to be afeared.'

He bent down to take a closer look at the woman, and then he saw the blood. Almost without thought he grabbed for his whistle and blew on it with all his might. Lights went on in windows across the street, and he heard someone raise a window nearby. A man came running across Houston.

'What's wrong?' he shouted.

'Run over to Mulberry Street as fast as you can,' McCabe shouted back. 'Tell them to send help over here right away.

And an ambulance!'

'Yessir!' the man said, and was off down the middle of Houston as if pursued by devils. People were coming out of the houses nearby, craning to see in the darkness.

The woman on the sidewalk groaned and her eyes opened. She saw McCabe bending over her, and they widened with terror that faded as she saw the shield with its New York City coat of arms and the number 486 above it.

'Police?' she sighed.

'That's right, lady,' McCabe said. 'Keep still, now. I've sent for help.'

'It was him,' she said.

'Who?'

'That murderer. The Ripper. Aaaaaaah.'

McCabe felt her clutch at his hand with her grubby talons. She was about thirty, he reckoned, and the marks of her profession were easy enough to spot: the cheap, shoddy clothes chosen for brightness rather than wear, the spots of rouge on the pasty cheeks, the dark circles beneath the tightly shut eyes.

'Are you — are you hurt bad?' he

asked. He could hardly lift up her clothes on the street and look. Besides, he didn't think he ought to. Even if she was a whore.

'Oh, he cut me, he cut me,' she wailed. 'Oh, bad, bad, he cut me.'

'There's an ambulance coming,' McCabe told her. 'Lie still now.'

As if they had heard him over at Headquarters, he heard the clanging of the bell six blocks away.

'But I cut him, too,' she said, with conviction.

'Yes,' he said. 'Try to keep still, try not to move.'

'Cut him,' she said.

'Good,' he said, wondering whether she knew what she was saying. 'What's your name, lady?'

'Tilly,' she said. 'Matilda Ball.'

'Where do you live, Tilly?'

'Rooming house, aaaaaah.' Her hand tightened convulsively on her wrist.

He heard the ambulance clearly now, bell ringrangring-rangringring, clattering across Broadway. People were looking up the street to see it coming.

'Where — where did it happen, Tilly?' he asked her.

'Back there.' Her breath was coming faster now, shallower. 'Ohhhh, ohhhh,' she moaned.

'Where, Tilly, where?'

'Ohhh,' she moaned. 'He cut me, oh, he cut me bad. My belly's on fire.'

'Tilly, try to listen. You want us to catch him, don't you?'

'Ohhhhaaaaaaah. He — it was him. Behind the hat shop.'

'Knox's? You mean behind Knox's hat shop?'

The woman didn't answer. She was unconscious as the ambulance came thundering over the cobbles of Houston Street, the horses rearing back as they were pulled to a halt when the driver saw McCabe's waving lantern.

'Get her to a doctor, fast!' he shouted to the two orderlies who jumped out of the back of the wagon with a rolled stretcher in their hands. 'And — oh, Frank, it's you. I was just — '

'Carry on, Jim,' O'Connor said. 'You're doing fine.'

'You take care of her,' McCabe shouted to the hospital men, as they loaded the wounded woman into the ambulance. 'Don't you lose her, now. She's seen the Ripper!'

'What did you get?' O'Connor asked McCabe. 'Anything?'

The ambulance pulled away from the sidewalk and whammed round the corner of Wooster, the driver thrashing the horses into a gallop even as the lurching conveyance rocked upright again. As the sound died away McCabe took O'Connor's arm and hurried him along Houston towards Broadway.

'Tilly Ball, her name is,' he said, not slackening his pace for a moment. 'Said it was the Ripper. Said he cut her bad.'

'How badly?'

'I couldn't tell, sir. But she was bleeding heavily.'

'What else?'

'She said that she cut him, too. I don't know if she knew what she was talking about.'

'Did she say where this happened?'

'She said 'behind the hat shop'. There's

253

only one hat shop on Houston, and that's Knox's. A block over.'

A man came down the steps of one of the houses and stood in front of them so they had to stop.

'What happened?' he said.

'Go on inside,' McCabe said.

'Wait,' O'Connor told him. 'Did you see anything?'

'Saw that woman reeling along the street,' the man said. 'Thought she was drunk until I heard the scream. Then the ambulance.'

'Did you see where she came from?'

'Up East, is all,' the man said.

'See anything else?'

'Else?'

'A man running? Anything like that?'

'No. Wait — yes. A man. Well, not running. Sort of hopping, like he had a limp. Went across Houston up there by the hat shop.'

'Thank you, sir,' O'Connor said. 'Jim, get this gentleman's name and address. We may want to talk to you again, sir,' he explained.

'Sure,' the man said, turning to give

McCabe his name and address as O'Connor ran flat out up the street to the doorway of the hat shop. It was a small place, no more than a fifteen-foot frontage, with a deep recessed doorway. The door of the shop itself was protected by one of those pull-down metal trellises. The recessed doorway had a tiled floor with a mosaic advertisement for stetson hats. It was splattered with blood. O'Connor bent down and touched the blood with his finger. It wasn't even sticky yet. The smell was hardly noticeable.

'Fresh,' he said to himself as McCabe came pounding up. He swung his lantern high and they saw for the first time that there was blood on the ledge of the window beside the door, and also a long, thin, but heavy smear of blood about waist-high across the wooden panelling to the right. O'Connor put his hand out flat against the level of the smear and then brought it back against his own body. It was just below his rib-cage.

'That has to have been from our killer,' he said. 'Unless he cut the woman around the chest somewhere.'

'I couldn't be sure, Frank,' McCabe confessed. 'But there's no blood on my uniform and I did sort of have her cradled in my arms.'

'All right,' O'Connor said. 'Here comes the patrol wagon.'

The horse-drawn wagon with eight patrolmen in it came blundering up Houston and McCabe stepped out to the edge of the sidewalk and waved it to a stop.

'Get this place roped off,' O'Connor told them. 'Two men on it until further notice. The store is not to be opened. One of you men get back to the station and see if they can get a surgeon over here. I want samples taken of the blood. Look smart, now!'

The men moved urgently to do his bidding, and O'Connor went over to Jim McCabe. He put his hand on the patrolman's shoulder.

'Third time lucky, hey, Jim?' he said.

'It'd be nice to think so,' said McCabe. He wasn't feeling the slightest bit fed up any more.

He is hurt.

Niemand is hurt.

There is blood running down his side.

The stinking whore bitch had a knife, the stinking whore bitch of Babylon had a knife and she hurt Niemand.

There is a strange, loose feeling in his stomach. As if something is cut.

The whore bitch had a knife.

Just as he was ready to do it, ready lightly, deftly to slash right to left and skip back, the sudden inner rigidity.

It was not possible.

Her eyes were wide, staring.

Then the rigidity slipped away and there was warmth.

Spreading.

Niemand may die.

No.

He is Nemesis. He cannot die.

A doctor?

Later. Niemand says later. First see how badly he is hurt.

In the safe place.

Up the stairs.

Where the newspapers which emblazoned his triumphs are pasted on the walls.

'POLICE BAFFLED.'

Where am I?

Spring Street?

Why is Niemand sitting on the sidewalk in Spring Street? This is not the safe place. The safe place is in the other direction. What is wrong with him?

He is hurt.

Oh. Ohhhhhhhhhhh. Oh. Agony?

Is that what they feel like? Is that the pain of which they die?

There is blood on Niemand's hands. On his clothes.

He must hide. And soon.

11

Tilly Ball was a Catholic, which probably saved her life.

Had she been a Presbyterian, the ambulance driver might have taken her up to the new Presbyterian Hospital on 71st Street, or at least as far as Bellevue on East 26th. The other choice might have been St Luke's, 54th and Fifth, but it wouldn't have mattered, because the jouncing, swaying, headlong journey would have undoubtedly killed her before she got near any one of them.

Instead she was taken to the Roman Catholic Hospital of St Vincent at the corner of 7th Avenue and 11th Street, a small, 250-bed affair run by the nuns of St Francis and St Vincent.

With a tenderness and care conditioned not by preconditioned reflexes about Tilly's status, her profession or her purse, but only by the fact that she was terribly, bloodily hurt, they washed her grubby body and cleansed her wounds as best they could and took her to the operating theatre.

The young doctor working there was not paid for the work he did. He had his own practice uptown, and it was a growing and successful one. Most of his cases were the removal of bunions from the feet of rich old ladies who lived in over-stuffed mansions on the Avenue or alongside the Park. To make some kind of amends for such a trivial waste of a God-given talent he worked three nights every week in St Vincent's. He was a very fine surgeon indeed, and he saved Tilly Ball's life with the same concern for her and her savaged body that he would have shown had she been a Vanderbilt or a Gould heiress literally worth her weight in gold.

A policeman was sent across from Mulberry Street an hour after Tilly arrived at the hospital, his duty to report immediately to Detective O'Connor whether she would live, and if so, the doctor's estimate of when he would be able to talk to the woman.

The answers, when they came were yes, and in about twenty-four hours. Perhaps tomorrow morning, the patrolman added, meaning tonight.

'How is she, Doc?' he asked the young surgeon when he arrived.

'Very low,' the young man said. 'She lost a great deal of blood.'

'What exactly were her wounds?'

'Do you have to know that?'

'Doc, you don't think I'd want to know if I didn't, do you?'

The surgeon, whose name was Francis Bennett, looked at O'Connor levelly for a long moment. Then he nodded, as if he had come to a decision.

'She was cut — very clumsily — with some very sharp instrument. There were three incisions running in a diagonal direction from the left side of the pubis to just beneath the right breast.'

'Three separate cuts?'

'I can't say. Possibly they were the result of one upward cut which might have been impeded by the woman's clothing. The deepest of the three cuts was the lower one, which had penetrated

261

the subcutaneous tissues and severed the muscles of the lower abdomen. A couple of millimetres more and he'd have disembowelled her.'

'That all?'

'All? I should think that would be enough for most people, Mr O'Connor!'

'Sorry, Doc. I meant, did you examine her clothing?'

'No. I put it all to one side. I imagined you people would want to look it over.'

'Thanks. Can I see her now?'

'Yes, but only for a little while. And don't get her excited. Those cuts are very deep and very dangerous.'

'I won't,' O'Connor promised, as the doctor accompanied him to the simple ward on the upstairs floor. It was all painted stark white, and the floors were shined well enough to give off reflections of the furniture standing on them. You'd have a hard life being a germ here, O'Connor thought. A silent nun preceded them into the ward and pushed aside the screens surrounding Tilly Ball's bed. She was lying with her eyes wide open, staring at the ceiling sightlessly.

'Tilly,' the doctor said.

Her eyes swivelled round, and a faint smile touched her lips.

'This is Detective O'Connor, Tilly. He wants to talk to you.'

O'Connor nodded and smiled at the girl. She was as white as the starched sheets she was lying between. There was a huge bump in the centre of the bed, where a cage was keeping the clothes off her stomach.

'I feel as if I'm in a little house,' she said.

'Nice and comfortable, though,' O'Connor grinned.

'I'll leave you to talk,' the doctor said. 'Call me if you need anything.'

His look emphasized the last word: he meant call me if anything happens *at all*.

'Feel well enough to talk, Tilly?' O'Connor asked.

'Guess so,' she said.

'Shall I ask you questions, or would you rather tell me in your own words what happened?'

'You ain't goin' to send me up, are you?' she asked.

'No, of course not. It's the man who attacked you, that's who we want.'

'Bastard!' she said, her lips clamping into a thin line. 'Tried to do for me, 'e did. But I give him one 'e didn't expect.'

'Tell me from the beginning.'

'Well,' she said. 'It was, like, you know, gettin' on in the morning. Half past three. Hardly anybody about any more, even on Broadway. I'd decided to call it a day, get off home.'

'To 33 Leroy Street?'

'That's r — 'ere, how did you know that?'

'It's on your record sheet, Tilly,' he said.

'Oh, of course,' she said. 'I forgot. Bein' in 'ere, you know. Don't seem right for a girl like me. Still. They're saints, ain't they? Seen it all and gone on to better things, God bless them.'

'You were thinking of going home. And then?'

'Out of nowhere up pops this jo — gent.'

'Gent?'

'Well, not really,' she said.

'Describe what he looked like.'

'Tall, 'e was. About five nine or so. Big around the shoulders. Good face, quite good lookin' really. Black hair, far as I could tell. His eyes . . . '

'His eyes?'

'I was just rememberin',' she said. 'Uhhhhhhuhhhh.' A theatrical little shiver. 'Bright blue they was. I seen them in the doorway. Blazin' bright blue.'

'How old would you say he was, Tilly?'

'Forty, maybe. Hard to tell at that age. They all look somewhere between thirty-five and fifty-five. But say forty.'

'What was he wearing?'

'Overcoat. Dark colour. That soft stuff.'

'Cashmere?'

'No, the stuff that feels like a cuddly puppy.'

'Crombie, you mean?'

'Crombie overcoat, that's right,' she said. 'Dark brown, black, I couldn't rightly tell you.'

'Anything else?'

'Not as I recall.'

'His hands — any rings on his fingers?'

'No. Definite.'

'Did he limp, or walk strangely in any way?'

'No, why?'

'Never mind. He came up to you in the street?'

'Yes. Y'don't think I — oh, bugger, o' course you do. No, listen, really, I was just decidin' whether to go home or not an' up pops this fellow. Like he came up out of an 'ole in the ground, know what I mean? 'Hello, ducks,' I sez. 'Give me quite a start, you did.''

'Where exactly was this, Tilly?'

'On Broadway, like I told you. On the corner of 'ouston Street.'

'You're sure?'

'Course I am. Not ten minutes before that I'd been lookin' at the jools in Ball & Blacks, hadn't I? Then I walked up the block one last time. He must've been standin' around the corner of 'ouston Street, waitin' for me.' Again she shivered, this time not theatrically.

'Did he speak?'

'Course he spoke. 'I'm sorry,' 'e sez, nice as you please. 'I was waiting for you.''

'What kind of voice? Deep, level, high?'

'Ordinary. Not deep. Just a man's voice.'

'Any accent?'

'Not as I noticed.'

'And then?'

'Well.' Tilly hesitated for a moment, then plunged in, her head down. ''Lookin' for some fun, then?' I asks him. 'Why not,' 'e sez. 'If you're free, that is.' Funny question, I thought. Still, it was late, an' I wasn't in no mood to worry. 'Oh, I'm free all right,' I sez. 'Nobody's waiting for you?' he sez. 'No,' I sez.'

'Are you sure he said it like that, Tilly?'

'Eh? How'd you mean?'

'He said, 'Nobody's waiting for you?' ?'

'That's what I just told you.'

'No, Tilly. I mean, did he say, 'Nobody's waiting for you.'' O'Connor put all the emphasis on the first word.

''ere,' Tilly said, her eyes widening. 'Now you come to mention it, that's just 'ow he did say it. 'Nobody's waiting for you.''

'You see why I'm asking.'

'O' course,' she said, softly. 'O' course.

267

Nobody. That's what 'e said.'

'Anyway, what happened then?'

'Well, we sorted out about the money. Gave me five dollars, 'e did.'

'And then?'

'I asked if 'e wouldn't like to come back to my place for the night, or we could both go to where 'e lived if he liked. Five dollars extra for the night, I told 'im. 'No, no,' he sez. 'Somewhere quiet and dark.''

'So you went to the doorway of Knox's.'

'That's right.'

'Did he say anything on the way?'

'No, nothing. It was like 'e was in a hurry, know what I mean?'

'Sure.'

'Well, we gets to the doorway. I hikes up me skirt, you know, and then, well. I can't tell you what 'appens next. Something, somehow, tells me. Funny,' she mused. 'It was like all the 'airs on the back of me 'ead was liftin' up. I *knew* it was 'im. I just knew it.'

'What happened?'

'I seen his 'and. I seen something

gleam. It was like it was all 'appening very slow, like in a dream. I knew 'e was goin' to cut me. I couldn't shout, or scream or anything. It was . . . '

'Take it steady, Tilly,' O'Connor said. 'If it's too much, I'll come back tomorrow.'

'No,' she spat venomously. 'I want 'im caught, Mr O'Connor! He *cut* me, the bastard. But I cut him, too.'

'You had a knife?'

'Lots o' the girls 'ave,' she explained. 'When them other two was done, lots of the girls started carryin' something. Some've got little revolvers, or derringers tucked in their purses. Me, I had a knife. Bought it down on the waterfront, one of them ship chandlers. It straps on your leg like a garter.'

'So, you saw — or felt — he was going to attack you. What did you do then?'

'I pulled out me knife and stuck it in him. There,' she said, pointing to O'Connor's middle.

'Here?' he said, pointing at the level of his diaphragm.

'More to the side,' she said. 'There, like.'

She touched him at about the point where his fourth rib was.

'Go on.'

'Then he cuts me. I could feel it. It was — '

'You don't have to describe that, Tilly. Tell me what happened next.'

'It's . . . it's all right,' she said. 'He pushed me back against the window. I don't know what happened. Next thing I know, I'm on the floor. I can feel blood all on my legs. Him, 'e falls back against the other side of the doorway — '

'Where the woodwork is?'

'That's it, sort of lurches sideways and out on the sidewalk. 'Whore of Babylon!' 'e shouts. 'Scarlet whore bitch of Babylon.' An' then he goes as if to come at me again. I sort of crawls, scrambles, like, out of the doorway and gets to my feet, I don't know how. Then I screams at the top of me voice and runs. And then the copper come around the corner. That's all I remember.'

She sank back on the pillow, her face strained and pale, her breathing shallow. There were beads of perspiration on her upper lip and she looked as if she might cry. O'Connor stood up and signalled to one of the nuns, who came over swiftly on soft feet. She looked at him reproachfully and shooed him away from the bed, pulling the screens closed behind her.

O'Connor stood there like a fool for several minutes, listening to the sound of faint movements. Then the nun came through the gap in the screens.

'I think that's more than enough, Mr O'Connor,' she said. 'I'll show you downstairs.'

'Thank you,' he said humbly.

'Will you want to see Dr Bennett before you leave?'

'I think not, sister,' O'Connor said.

'You'll find there's a box by the door if you feel you'd like to give something to help us in our work,' the nun said.

O'Connor did the best he could to manufacture a smile, and went through the door feeling as if her eyes were burning holes in his back.

★　★　★

The newspapers really had a field day with the attempt to murder Tilly Ball. Her picture, a drawing that had been made at the bedside by an agency artist, was on every front page, along with a plethora of detail about her gallant fight with the maniac killer. There were plenty of illustrations for the papers to print. There was Tilly's knife, found by the police in the gutter halfway down Greene Street. There was the doorway of Knox's hat shop, the bloodstained floor and walls 'reconstructed' by staff artists to resemble something one might have expected in an abattoir. There was stout-hearted Patrolman McCabe, the hero of the hour, who had surprised the assassin (a piece of news that came as some surprise to McCabe himself) at his awful work. There were the mysterious bloodstains that had been found at the foot of a wall in Spring Street, not far from the junction with Greene. There were the speculations of eminent medical men, fatly fee'd by the tsars of Printing House Square, upon the extent and nature of the wound or wounds Tilly Ball might have inflicted upon her would-be assassin.

Most of it, as always, was hogwash, balderdash, drivel, tommyrot, bosh, tosh, tripe, bilge or piffle. In other words, hot air. The only useful thing in all the papers, as far as the Detective Corps was concerned, was the fact that the description of the man, with the additional details Tilly Ball had supplied, was prominently printed in every one. Together with the suggestion (provided by the Detective Corps) that any employer having on his pay-roll someone answering the description who had not turned up for work in the last two days should immediately contact the police. Any wife whose husband was away from home without warning was asked to do likewise. Any doctor who was called or asked to treat any kind of knife wound was requested to advise the police. Any hotel-keeper, lodging-house-owner, apartment-keeper or tenement landlord who had a tenant answering the description whom he had not seen in the last two or three days was bidden to call in at the nearest station house, where his visit would be kept confidential.

All of which, of course, resulted in a massive inundation of information from people who had lodgers with peculiar habits, employers with employees given to arbitrary absenteeism, wives with errant husbands, not to mention wives, sweethearts and lovers who had reason to suspect that perhaps their cutie-pie baby might have a roaming disposition. It was the responsibility of the Detective Corps to check every single one of these reports, while at the same time following up their own lines of investigation. For instance, every hospital, benevolent, charity or private, had to be checked. The Detective Corps was too wise in the ways of its city to believe that every doctor in Manhattan was public-spirited enough to come forward voluntarily if he had treated someone for a knife wound, so they checked them all, anyway. All the missions, all the hostels, and all the barber shops — there were plenty of barbers with a rudimentary knowledge of anatomy, and enough rough medical experience to put half a dozen catgut stitches through the lips of a knife-wound. Down on Water Street, for instance, there were knife fights every day of the week. If you got stuck, as long as it was in a non-vital spot, odds were the barber could sew you up. As long as you didn't die of blood poisoning or gangrene you would probably pull through.

And to be on the safe side, every stiff, every floater, every suicide and fatal accident case was checked over at the morgue on East 26th.

Nothing. One day.

Hospitals, clinics, missions, flop-houses, hostels and barber shops.

Nothing. Two days.

Over four hundred reports from various precinct houses turned in by public-spirited (or malicious, or suspicious, or mischievous) citizens.

Nothing. Three days.

And then Detective Billy McLaughlin came up with an idea.

Why, not, he said, make a list of all the names from the reports filed at the various station houses in every precinct, and check them out with the Department of Missing Persons?

Why?

Well, he explained, if the same name appeared twice, it could be that they would have a genuine lead from two directions, rather than (as in most cases) a dead end in one. For instance, if a coal-merchant in the lower East Side had reported one of his men not having turned up for work, it was checked out. The man's home was visited. He was either home sick, or accountable for. But what if Niemand was from out of town? Maybe someone who lived in New Jersey, or Brooklyn? All such cases, he said, were being passed to the appropriate police authority for checking out locally. That might take weeks — the Brooklyn and New Jersey boys weren't going to break their asses trying to pick up Manhattan's broken eggs. As and when they got round to it, they'd check. As and when.

Well, everyone said, unenthusiastically, it's an idea.

McLaughlin went ahead with it and came up covered in glory. A printer with a business at 1877 Broadway had reported that his senior compositor, Peter Fisher, had not turned up for work the morning after the attempted murder, or since. The printer's name was Henry Chancellor, and the description he gave of Fisher was very close to that of Niemand. He said, though, that Fisher was in every way a model employee, who could quote at length from any portion of the Bible, and was happily married and clean-living.

In Missing Persons McLaughlin found that a Mrs Henrietta Fisher, of 355 Laurel Road, Hoboken, New Jersey (just across the North River), had filed only the day before a request with the Department to try to locate her husband, Peter, who had been missing since — and here he shouted the date triumphantly — the day before the attempted murder of Tilly Ball.

'So what does that give us?' Inspector Byrnes asked him. He was fond of Billy McLaughlin, and respected the Irishman's hunches — as an Irishman himself, he had great sympathy for intuition.

'Well, sor,' McLaughlin said. 'It gives us a man answering perfectly to the description of Niemand, who's not turned up for work and not turned up at home and not been accounted for elsewhere.'

'So,' Byrnes said. 'All we have to do now is find him.'

McLaughlin sat there and looked at his Chief, crestfallen.

'Yes, sor,' he said. 'That's all.'

'All right,' Byrnes said, more to cheer him up than anything else. 'Why don't you go over to Hoboken and talk to Mrs Fisher?'

There was no way he could know it, of course, but that was one of the smartest decisions he was going to make this side of Christmas. Maybe he had a little Irish working for him on the side himself, at that.

★   ★   ★

'What finally decided you to go to the Missing Persons Bureau, Mrs Fisher?' McLaughlin asked sympathetically. He felt sorry for this dowdy, middle-aged woman with the worn hands, living in a run-down frame house on one of the poorer streets in Hoboken.

'I — I don't know,' she said. She was struggling not to cry, and he turned and looked out of the window while she got control of herself.'

'He — never stayed away this long before,' she finally managed.

'He stays away regularly, then?'

'No,' she said. 'Only this last month or two.'

'How long does he normally stay away?'

'Oh, just overnight. He would say in the morning before he went to work that he had business in the city that night, and to save having to rush for the last ferry he'd take a cheap room somewhere and stay over.'

'Do you know where he usually stayed?'

'No, I'm afraid not.'

'Can you recall the dates when he stayed in Manhattan?'

'I — I think so. I'm not sure.'

'Mrs Fisher, I have the feeling you suspected something was wrong with your husband. Did you?'

'Well,' she said hesitantly. 'I thought . . . I was sure . . . I was sure there was another woman in New York!'

The words came all of a rush, and McLaughlin waited and said nothing.

'I didn't know what to do,' she said. 'How can a wife fight that sort of thing? I know there are young girls in the city who will — who will, well, go with a man if he shows them a good time. There were the things I found, you see. The — '

'What things?' said McLaughlin sharply.

'A woman's handkerchief,' she said, in a low voice. 'And a hair slide. I found them in his overcoat. He never mentioned them, although I felt sure he knew they were gone.'

'What did you do with them?'

'I — I burned them,' she said defiantly.

'Mrs Fisher,' McLaughlin said reproachfully.

'I — I put them away. I was going to confront him with them. If he stayed away again. Then he. Then he — '

That was as far as she could go. She slumped into a chair, weeping softly.

There is very little a detective can do at a time like this. Although his normal human reaction is to try to console the stricken person, such an act, laudable in an unofficial capacity, becomes dangerous in an official one — as the many officers who have been accused of attempted rape would willingly testify. You pat a shoulder, loan a handkerchief or provide, either metaphorically or literally, a shoulder to cry on, and the result is likely to be a bundle of trouble you could have done without. Ask any insurance salesman about widows.

After a while, if you're a cop, you get a slight callousing of the emotional responses, anyway. So you stand there, as McLaughlin was standing now, turning your hat-brim round and round between your fingers, waiting until the sobbing stops. Then when it finally does stop you pick up where you left off.

'You believe your husband has run off with another woman, Mrs Fisher?'

She nodded, dabbing at reddened eyes with a tiny, lace-trimmed handkerchief.

'Have you any idea who the woman

might be, where they might go?'

She shook her head.

'Did your husband take any clothes with him? Pack a suitcase, an overnight bag, anything like that?'

'No,' she said. 'All his clothes are still here.'

'Then it hardly seems likely — '

' — what else could it be?' she burst out. 'What else?'

'Could be a lot of other things besides another woman, Mrs Fisher,' McLaughlin said. She looked at him gratefully, as if it was what she had wanted to hear.

'That hair slide and handkerchief you say you found,' he said. 'Could I see them?'

'Of course,' she said. 'If you'll just wait a minute.' She was glad to get out of the room for a moment, which was why he had asked her for the things. He had felt the air had turned a little cooler, realized that she was not the kind of woman who liked to display her emotions in front of a stranger. Perhaps not at all, he thought.

He looked round the room.

There was a velveteen-covered sofa on

the wall beneath the window that looked out on to the street. Matching velveteen drawing curtains and patterned lace window curtains inside them. A round table in the middle of the room, four chairs set round it. There was a large oil lamp on the table, with a neat lace doiley beneath it. On each side of the high-mantelled fireplace were two high-backed armchairs, an imitation carriage clock in the centre of the mantel, small vases with drooping flowers in them at each end. On the wall behind him a framed print of Landseer's 'Stag at Bay' over a heavy sideboard with two silver candelabra on it. Between the candelabra was a thick, leather-bound bible. McLaughlin glanced at it: it was open at *The Revelation of St John*. Against the wall opposite the window was a rosewood piano, a long thin lace runner on top, family photographs facing inwards from both sides. There was a wedding photograph — Fisher and his wife, McLaughlin guessed — taken perhaps twenty-five years earlier. She had been no beauty, but pretty enough in her long smooth white silk gown, slim and dark, eyes wide with the wonder of being a wife. Fisher looked impassive: just a tall, dark, good-looking young man in a claw-hammer coat. There were photographs of children: a girl and a younger boy. An older picture of a man and a woman, the man posed rigidly at the seated woman's right shoulder, his derby at a carefully held right angle to his shoulder line. A head and shoulders picture of a man who — McLaughlin looked closer: of course! Fisher! It was an older version of the face in the wedding photograph.

Then Mrs Fisher came back into the room with a small wooden box in her hands. It was upholstered inside, and had small trays lined with flowered material. Her sewing box? Jewel box? he thought, as he watched her lay it down on the table in front of him.

The hairslide was a cheap one, imitation tortoiseshell; and the handkerchief plain white cotton with neither initials nor laundry mark.

Ah, well, he thought. No miracles today.

'Is that a photograph of your husband, Mrs Fisher?' he asked.

'Yes, he had it taken last year.'

'May I borrow it?'

'Of course. You'll take — '

' — care of it? Of course. Tell me, does Mr Fisher speak any languages?'

'Yes. Well, that is to say, a little German. His grandfather was from Germany, you see.'

'Are those your children in the photograph?'

'Yes — many years ago, of course. James is married and lives in Baltimore. Edwina lives in Philadelphia. Her husband is in the banking business there. She's expecting a baby any day now.'

'Getting back to your husband, Mrs Fisher,' McLaughlin said. 'Does he own a crombie overcoat?'

'A — ?'

'Crombie overcoat.'

'Why . . . yes, if you mean that sort of nubby wool material.'

'Black?'

'Yes. Why? What? Has someone seen him?'

'It's possible, Mrs Fisher,' McLaughlin said. 'That's why I want to borrow the photograph.'

'Where? Where was he seen?'

'If it was your husband,' McLaughlin said levelly. 'In Manhattan.'

'Was he alone?' He looked at her, sorry for what he was going to have to do now.

'No,' he said. 'He was seen with a prostitute.'

Something happened to her face. It was as if he had literally struck her and was watching the red mark throb into visibility. The side of her face turned a sort of mottled red and she breathed with a strange hissing, choking sound.

'Mrs Fisher?' he said, alarmed.

'Not that!' she hissed. 'Not that!'

McLaughlin kept silent and did not move. He did not know what was going on in the woman's mind, but he knew enough not to ask a question, not to disturb the upheaval she was undergoing.

Her eyes cleared as he watched and she turned on him, disdain in her voice.

'It could not have been my husband,' she said. 'It could *never have* been Peter!'

'What makes you so sure of that?' he asked her.

'Sit down, Mr McLaughlin,' the woman said. 'There is something you have to be told.'

There was a note of firm command, cold appraisal in her voice. He sat down in one of the armchairs and Mrs Fisher began to tell him about her husband.

12

In every bar, every saloon, every grog shop and cellar dive on the upper West Side, in every store and warehouse, every apartment house and tenement, copies of a 15 × 10 poster suddenly appeared. Literature it was not. But it said what it had to say with wickedly simple effect.

LAMENT FOR A TOUGH COP [it said in huge black print]

DENNIS O'SULLIVAN,
TOUGH AS CAN BE
HARD AS THE NAILS ON YOUR BOOT
WHERE IS YOUR WHISTLE
YOUR BADGE AND YOUR GUN
AND YOUR BEAUTIFUL POLICE-
    MAN'S SUIT?
WHERE ARE THE DUSTERS YOU
    PLANNED TO LOCK UP
SALT THEM AWAY TO A MAN?
TAKING A SMILE AT THE LOCAL

288

SALOON —
CATCH US, OLD BOY, IF YOU CAN!

(Signed) THE HUDSON DUSTERS.

Copies very soon found their way all over the city and this blatant disregard for the majesty of the law brought the full wrath of the four commissioners of police down like a falling house upon the head of Chief of Police James J. Kelso. They hauled him over the coals for every damned thing they could think of (and a few they invented) while they were chewing him out for letting a cheap street gang kick the bejeesus out of one of his patrolmen.

Chief of Police James Kelso was not a man to stand mutely by while manure was shovelled all over his reputation in sizeable quantities, and so he in turn proceeded to play merry hell with the digestion and equanimity of the four inspectors who were jointly responsible for the sixty-four precincts in New York City, and especially did he play merry hell with the peacefully flatulent life of

Inspector Michael Dempsey, whose specific area of command included the Charles Street station house.

Dempsey, being an imaginative man, immediately hauled in Captain Terence Mulhern, in charge of Charles Street, and in language which he certainly had not learned from the Jesuit fathers who had been responsible for his education and upbringing proceeded to take large strips from the defenceless hide of the unfortunate police captain.

Smarting under the double humiliation of being treated like a skivvy by the inspector, and also of knowing that every single police precinct captain in the city was aware of his disgrace, Mulhern paraded every man in the Charles Street station before him — sergeants, roundsmen and patrolmen alike, no man spared and no holds barred — and tore them off a strip the like of which few of them had suffered during their entire career with New York's finest.

Dennis O'Sullivan, the captain told them in ringing tones, had been a good cop, a brave cop, an intrepid cop, an honest cop. For his pains he had been reduced to a shambling wreck of a human being who would be lucky if he could get a job as a night watchman on some quiet dock in Poughkeepsie. Meanwhile, the Hudson Dusters were walking round his patch — *his patch!* — with chips on their shoulders the size of small logs, daring any cop in New York to knock them off.

Well, by God, they weren't going to get away with it, he told them. Every man in this goddamned station house was going to go out and knock the teeth out of any Duster he ran across on the streets. He was going to haul in any Duster he saw so much as spitting on the sidewalk. He was going to crack the head of any Duster he heard utter a swear word. He was going to break the stranglehold those cocky sonsofbitches had on the upper West Side, or he was going to have the guts of every man jack in front of him for garters, and did they understand him?

Yes, sir, they chorused dutifully to a man.

Well, then, he told them, don't just stand there like dumb oxes! Get out and get on with it!

'Yes, *sir*,' they snapped, coming to attention and saluting.

Of course, this was all for the record, and for the newspapers, several representatives of whose power were recording the proceedings at Charles Street. 'A wave of arrests,' they announced to the populace, 'is expected shortly. Captain Mulhern has declared war upon the vicious hoodlums who infest the city streets. The gauntlet he has flung down will not, of course, be picked up by these cowardly deadbeats, these cheap thugs, these shop-robbing rapscallions.'

They had a good laugh about that down on Greenwich Street.

Hoodlums, eh? Deadbeats, thugs, rapscallions, eh?

They awaited, without terror, the promised wave of arrests. Meanwhile they got on with the more interesting — and rewarding — business of life: knocking people on the head, stealing the Hudson River Railroad blind, lifting whatever could be lifted from the docks, swiping convertible paper from the offices of stockbrokers and the thousand other little rackets that they had been successfully operating for several decades and would no doubt go on operating for several more.

Life went on in the upper West Side.

After all, what was one tough cop more or less?

★　★　★

'Should we put someone on the house?' Byrnes asked.

'Already done, Chief,' McLaughlin said. 'The local station will keep a twenty-four-hour watch, and advise us if he shows up.'

'But you don't think he will?'

'No, I don't.'

'Reasons?'

'What I already told you, Chief. The wife's story checks out. God, she must have hated that old lady!'

'The doctor confirmed it?'

'Yes, he did. Dr James Fraser,'

McLaughlin said, referring to his note-book. '187 West 68th. He put 'heart failure' on the death certificate at Fisher's request. But there's no question as to the real cause of death, and he'll testify to it if necessary.'

'So you think that gives us motive?'

'Well, doesn't it, sir? Here's Fisher, who worships his mother above all women — constantly telling his wife how much better she'd be if she were more like his mother. And then the old lady confesses to him that she's dying of advanced syphilis. And that his father gave it to her.'

'You're guessing.'

'No, sir. That's what his wife told me. You should have heard the satisfaction in her voice when she told me what the old lady died of and how she got it.'

'And the mother died when?'

'The beginning of September.'

'Two weeks later, our Mr Niemand starts ripping street-walkers,' Byrnes said. 'What else?'

'The wife confirms the dates Fisher was away from home. They're the same: 18

294

and 25 September, and the day Tilly Ball was attacked.'

'It could all still be coincidence,' Byrnes said. 'No proof there at all.'

'It would have to be a hell of a coincidence, Chief.'

'There have been longer ones. What about the theory that he's taken off with some woman?'

'It doesn't fit. Look, Chief, here's a respectable married man, deacon in the church, two grown children, steady job, never missed a day's work in five years. Suddenly he ups and runs off with a woman whom he can't have known longer than three weeks. And that only three weeks after the death of his mother in the circumstances we've just discussed. It isn't likely, is it?'

'I didn't say it was likely,' Byrnes said doggedly. 'I said it was possible.'

'One other thing.'

'What's that?'

'Money,' said McLaughlin triumphantly. 'Fisher earns $200 a month before taxes. Out of that he kept $20 a week for his pocket money, fares, lunches, streetcars. You ever tried to keep a mistress on $20 a week, Chief?'

'I've never tried it at all,' said Byrnes stiffly. 'Maybe his old lady left him some money.'

'Old Mrs Fisher lived in an apartment on West 88th Street,' the detective said, referring to his notes again. 'Number 20. Two rooms full of broken-down old furniture even the local mission wouldn't be able to find much use for. She was a charity case.'

'Gambling, some other windfall?'

'Come on, Chief,' McLaughlin smiled. 'You're reaching.'

'Damned right,' said Byrnes.

'Listen,' McLaughlin said. 'I've got an idea where he may be.'

Byrnes raised his eyebrows, nothing more. Billy McLaughlin's first hunch had paid off in spades. Why not this one?

The detective unrolled a large-scale map of Manhattan on the desk, weighting it down at each corner with the inkwells from Byrnes's onyx desk set (presented by his precinct when he attained the rank of captain in 1867). On the map were three large crosses: one marking the place on West Third were Lily Purcell had been killed, a second on Spring for Katy Dawkins and a third on Houston at the spot where Knox's hat shop stood. They were almost in a straight north–south line. Round each cross McLaughlin had drawn a circle perhaps four inches in diameter. Each of the outer circles overlapped the central one top and bottom.

'What are the circles?' Byrne asked.

'Ten minutes' fast walking distance from the scene of the crimes,' McLaughlin said. 'I paced them out myself.'

'How d'you know our Fisher didn't run?'

'He might have done the first two times, Chief, but the third time he had a hole in his belly. If that was his blood that was found on Spring Street, it was a nasty one. He wouldn't have been running.'

'So?'

'With the first two murders the killer had all the time he needed to get away. The third attempt, however, he had hardly any time at all. We had men all over that area within fifteen minutes of the attack, yet they found no sign of the killer. Conclusion: he has a bolt-hole very close by.'

'We always figured that as a likelihood,' Byrnes said.

'The only two areas he could feasibly be in, then, are the two where the circles overlap,' McLaughlin said. 'With the emphasis being on the bottom one, because we know he was in Spring Street after he attacked Ball in Houston.'

'Know,' Byrnes said, softly, sarcastically.

'Guess, then,' McLaughlin said impatiently. 'My hunch is that he's in this area — seven blocks on each side of Prince Street.'

'So?'

'I want a door-to-door search of both those areas.'

'How many men?'

'Two squads of twenty men, a detective in charge of each.'

'Well,' Byrnes said slowly.

'Sir?'

'What the hell are you waiting for?' the inspector shouted.

'This policeman,' the old man said, using the word like the foulest curse, 'this *seccatura*, this pest, this detective. Where is he?'

'He has disappeared, Don Gabriele,' said the younger man sitting opposite him.

His voice was very soft, very respectful. He did not wish to arouse the anger of the old man. Sixty and some years Don Gabriele might be, slower now in his movements and sometimes a little halting in his speech, but he was still an immensely powerful man and only someone tired of life would voluntarily anger him.

'I see,' Don Gabriele said. 'You understand that this is a matter of the highest consequence, of course?'

'Of course, Don Gabriele,' the young man said. 'Of course.'

'You are my *consigliere*, my adviser, Nicholas,' Don Gabriele said. 'I rely upon your judgement. You tell me the man has disappeared, this *sporcizia*, this filth, who makes cripples of two of our people. You tell me you cannot find someone who threatens what we are trying to build. I do not criticize you, Nicholas. But I am puzzled. Is it that you do not have enough people to find him?'

'No, no,' Nicholas Morello told his Don. 'It isn't that. He's just gone to earth. Don't you worry, we'll find him.'

'I do not worry, Niccolò,' Don Gabriele said softly. '*You* worry.'

He let the words hang cold in the air for a moment. 'And our people, in the police? Can they discover nothing?'

'Only that Petrosino is officially on leave of absence, authorized by Byrnes of the Detective Corps. No one else knows anything.'

'Strange,' mused the old man. 'And untypical of them. They are usually so obvious. What is this Petrosino, a mad one, some kind of crusader, perhaps?'

'It's difficult to know,' Morello said. 'His parents are ordinary people. From Salerno. The father is Sicilian.'

'And he allows his son to do this?' Don Gabriele's eyebrows rose.

'The son is American born, Don Gabriele,' Morello said.

'Ah,' the old man sighed, as if that were explanation enough in itself.

'What then is your judgement, Niccolò?'

'I figure he's around somewhere, poking his nose into our thing,' Morello said. 'He speaks Italian, looks like one of us. He could be anywhere: on the docks, in the markets, on the streets — anywhere. We'll find him, though. It may take a while, but sooner or later we'll find him. Wherever he is, whatever name he's using. If he's in New York, we'll find him.'

'*No importa,*' the Don told him. 'It doesn't matter. There are other, more important things than this. Of course, Niccolò, you must find this policeman, and make an example of him. And I am confident that you will not fail me.'

Again he left the small, pregnant silence to build into a chilling threat.

'It is a small moment of freedom that Petrosino has,' the Don continued, 'but a small moment only. Let him enjoy it. We

301

have all the time in the world.'

He nodded and waved a languid hand. Morello got up from the chair opposite the old man's and went quietly out of the room. As he closed the door behind him he glanced back. Don Gabriele, *capo mafia*, undisputed ruler of Manhattan, was nodding in his chair, dreaming of playing *bocce* beneath the hot Sicilian sun in the dusty square of Piana dei Greci.

Morello nodded. The old man was right, as usual. Petrosino was hardly the most important thing they had to worry about right now. There were the *camorriste* in Brooklyn to consider: they were becoming more militant, more demanding. One day they would have to be reckoned with. As for Petrosino, as the Don said, *no importa*: one day, maybe not tomorrow or the day after, maybe not this year or next, but one day, he would be found. The whole thing was simply a matter of time and patience. And the Mafia had plenty of both.

★　★　★

They found Niemand on the second day.

It was a fleabag hotel at 359 Spring, a run-down four-storey affair that let rooms by the month without asking too many questions of its occupants. There was a desk clerk during the day, but at night the guests used their own keys to get in.

There was a standard procedure for this kind of search. Two patrolmen took each building, working their way through it apartment by apartment, room by room. They knocked on the door, one standing to one side of the door, revolver holster unfastened and his hand on the butt of his pistol, while the other asked the routine questions: who lives here, anybody missing, have you seen this man (show the photograph of Fisher), thank you very much, sorry to have bothered you.

The desk clerk at the Fountain Hotel — which was the grandiose name its original owner had given to the now moth-eaten, dingy twenty-room fleabag at 359 Spring — recognized the photograph immediately and told them that it was Mr Peter Rache, who had a room on the first floor back, he'd take them up. 'Stay put!' the patrolman told him, and ran out into Spring Street, blowing his whistle. Within a few minutes he had every man on the squad round the door, as well as a growing crowd of curious passers-by. Billy McLaughlin gave orders that three of the patrolmen should keep the crowd well back. Two others he sent round the back of the hotel. The others he posted in the lobby and on the stairway. Then he and two patrolmen went up the stairs to Room 12.

The corridor was dank and gloomy, the only light coming in through a small window at the end of the hallway.

'One of you on each side,' McLaughlin said, and knocked loudly on the door of No. 12.

'Police!' he shouted. 'Open up in there!'

A door opened down the hallway and someone poked a head round the jamb of the door, eyes wide. 'Stay back there,' snarled one of the patrolmen, and the door slammed as the head was hastily withdrawn. Inside the room McLaughlin thought he heard the creak of bedsprings but then there was silence. He hammered on the door.

'Open up!' he yelled. 'Or we'll break it down!'

He waited a moment, and when there was no reply he nodded to the patrolman on his right. Thomas Scott, Badge No. 487, drew his pistol, cocked it and fired a shot into the door lock. There was an ear-stunning, solid metallic 'whang!' and the corridor filled with powder smoke and the reek of cordite. McLaughlin leaned back against the corridor wall, braced himself and lashed out at the splintered door with the heel of his shoe. The door bowed but did not open.

'Bolted,' McLaughlin panted. 'Break it down!'

Scott and the other patrolman, Steve Garrett, Badge No. 512, got set, shoulders down across the narrow hall, and then they ran at the door together, smashing into it like locomotives, bursting it from its flimsy hinges. The door went in and down flat on the linoleum floor with a tremendous crash and the two patrolmen went over it, half off-balance, sprawling, hands reaching out to steady themselves. The room was in darkness and smelled bad, but McLaughlin saw the man in there moving crabwise away from the door, something in his hand catching a gleam of light from the grimy hallway window. Even as he formed a shout of warning one of the patrolmen shouted in pain and McLaughlin saw him clasp a hand to his face, blood spurting between the spread fingers.

'Watch out!' the detective yelled as the man kicked Patrolman Scott in the face and then came straight at McLaughlin with the open cut-throat razor held high, ready to slash at the Detective's face.

McLaughlin had no damned choice at all.

He shot the man down at a range of no more than three feet. In the confined space between them the sound of the shot was appallingly loud, and the force of the bullet lifted Fisher off his feet and smashed him back against the door jamb, shaking the flimsy walls with the impact.

The razor dropped from his hands, and his eyes bulged with astonishment and pain. He slid to his knees as Scott came out of the doorway and kicked the razor away from the still-questing fingers. McLaughlin heard the thunder of feet as his men came up the stairs, and he turned as they piled into the corridor, the pistol in his hand still smoking.

'Get an ambulance!' he shouted. 'Scott, get in there and see what you can do for Garrett!'

'You okay, Billy?' the patrolman panted.

'Fine. Go on, now!'

He knelt down and turned Fisher over. He was still breathing, but the front of his body was a pulsing mass of blood from the sternum to the groin. McLaughlin frowned: his shot had taken Fisher high on the centre of his chest, blackening the shirt-front, but it couldn't account for this kind of bleeding. He ripped the man's shirt open and sucked in his breath at what he saw. Below the rib-cage Fisher's belly was an angry, swollen pus-filled mess with a black and foetid mouth from which radiated striations of yellow-black and purple. Gangrene! Fisher had been all but dead on his feet as he came through the door.

Fisher's eyes flickered and then opened. He groaned, his groan softening into a sigh.

'What?' he whispered. 'What did?'

McLaughlin bent closer to catch the hissing words.

'What did you say, Fisher?' he said, harshly. 'What did you say?'

'Mother?' Fisher said. 'What did? You . . . '

'What did you what?'

'Tell me for?' Fisher sighed.

And then he was dead.

13

Everybody was pleased. The governor was pleased. The politicians were pleased. The mayor was pleased. The newspapers, especially, were pleased: they had a stand-by subject for features that would be good for reviving every couple of years with practically no rewrites at all. The streetwalkers were pleased because they could now get back on the streets and recoup the losses they had suffered during the time that the Ripper had frightened them off their beats. The Detective Corps were pleased because they had one less case to occupy them. The beat policemen were pleased because it was one less thing to watch out for. You might have thought that everyone would be happy, but of course, that wasn't so. Life was still just as real and earnest, and it went on whether there was one madman less in the world or not. The drunks still got drunk, the dips still lifted wallets, the confidence men still sold the Astor Hotel, the whores on Water Street still slipped the sailors chloral hydrate and tossed them out on to the sidewalks. The endless, pulsing, roaring life of Manhattan went on.

Inspector Thomas F. Byrnes sat in the mayor's office and listened to the fulsome phrases that were being showered upon his head. He didn't like the mayor. He didn't much like politicians of any kind, and city politicians were some degrees dirtier than most. Unfortunately he could not say this, since the mayor was also his boss. So he smiled and nodded and said as little as he could, waiting for a decent moment when he could rise, say goodbye and get back to the pile of work waiting for him at Mulberry Street.

'A fine record, Tom, fine,' the mayor was saying. 'The city is proud of you, proud of your men. Finest Detective Corps in the world.'

'Thank you, sir,' Byrnes said.

'You look restive, Tom,' the mayor said, sympathetically. 'Got a lot on?'

'Quite a bit,' Byrnes said.

'I know, I know,' the mayor sighed. 'We public servants . . . ' He sighed again and Byrnes smiled to himself. The mayor hadn't done an honest day's work in the last ten years, but that was by the bye.

'If there's nothing else, sir . . . ?' he said, rising.

'What? Oh, yes, of course. No, I don't think so, Tom. Think we've covered everything. Lots to do, lots to do, eh?'

'That's right, sir.' Byrnes said.

'Point taken,' the mayor said, and Byrnes concealed a grin. He got up to go, picking up his hat from the chair by the door.

'Oh, by the way, Tom,' the mayor said, as if in afterthought, 'how are you doing with that investigation into the, uh, secret society?'

'The Italian thing, you mean?'

'That's right. Maffeyo, or something.'

'Mafia, sir.'

'Anything breaking on that?'

'No,' said Byrnes quietly. 'But we're working on it.'